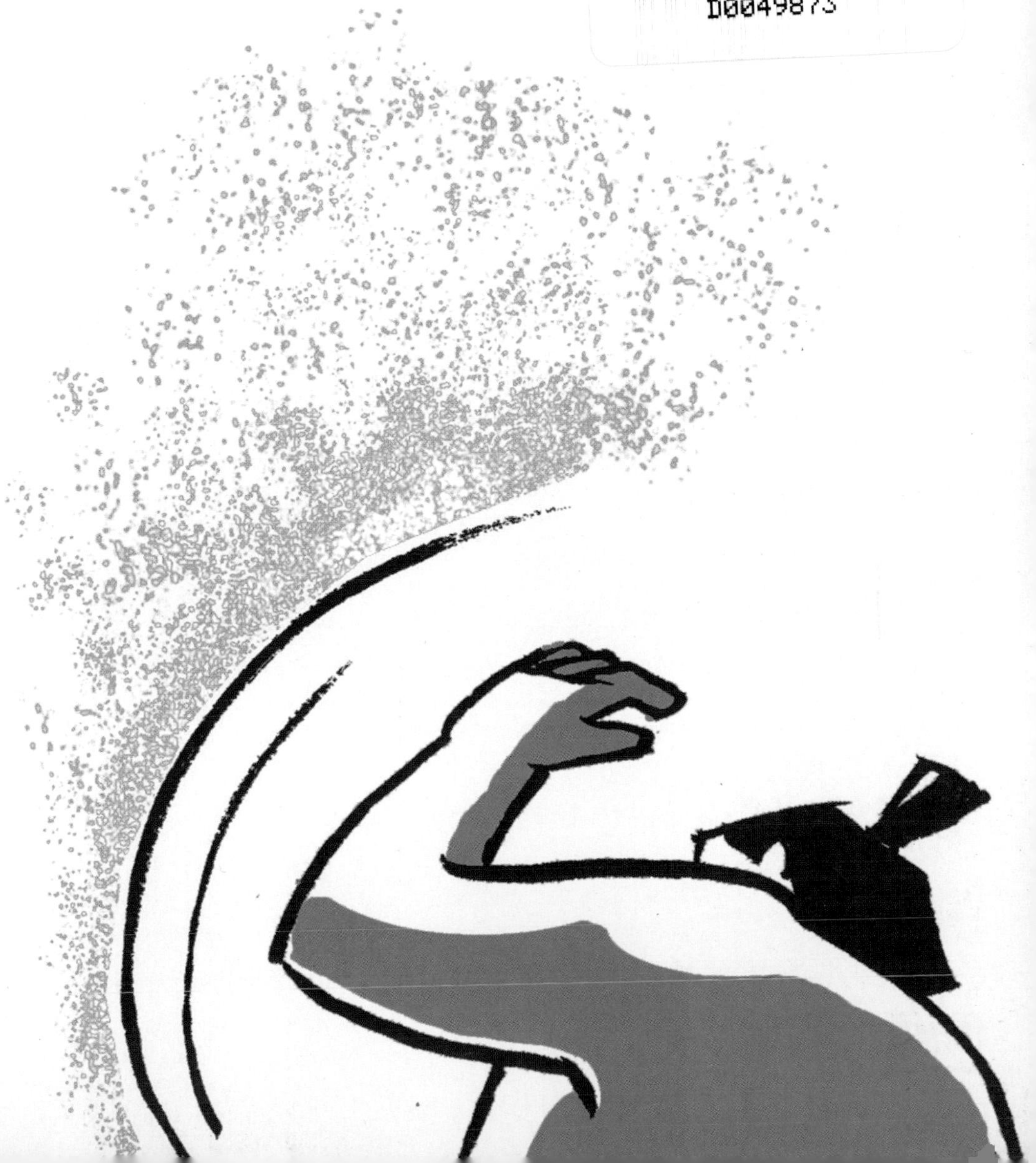

First Second

New York & London

Copyright © 2012 by Thien Pham

Published by First Second
First Second is an imprint of Roaring Brook Press,
a division of Holtzbrinck Publishing Holdings Limited Partnership
175 Fifth Avenue, New York, New York 10010

All rights reserved

Distributed in the United Kingdom by Macmillan Children's Books,
a division of Pan Macmillan.

Library of Congress Cataloging-in-Publication Data

Pham, Thien.
  Sumo / Thien Pham. — 1st ed.
      p. cm.
  Summary: A washed-up American football player finds a new life in sumo
wrestling.
  Summary: Scott, abandoned by his girlfriend and having lost his dream
of playing professional football, is offered a position in a Japanese
sumo training `stable,` where he seems to find himself again.
  ISBN 978-1-59643-581-0 (pbk.)
1. Graphic novels. [1. Graphic novels. 2. Sumo—Fiction. 3.
Americans—Japan—Fiction. 4. Self-realization—Fiction. 5.
Japan—Fiction.] I. Title.
  PZ7.7.P515Sum 2012
  741.5'952—dc23

                                        2012011298

First Second books are available for special promotions and premiums.
For details, contact: Director of Special Markets, Holtzbrinck Publishers.

FIRST
EDITION

First edition 2012
Design by Colleen AF Venable
Printed in China

10 9 8 7 6 5 4 3 2 1

THANK YOU:
Gene Yang
Jing Bentley
Mark Miyake
Briana Loewinsohn
Ryan Knight
Kenny Ferrari
Asami Salberry
Spencer Kawamoto
Annette Counts
Vihn Tran
Jesse Reklaw
Wahab Algarmi
Dylan Williams
Jason Shiga

SUMO
THIEN PHAM

:01

First Second
New York & London

For
Lark

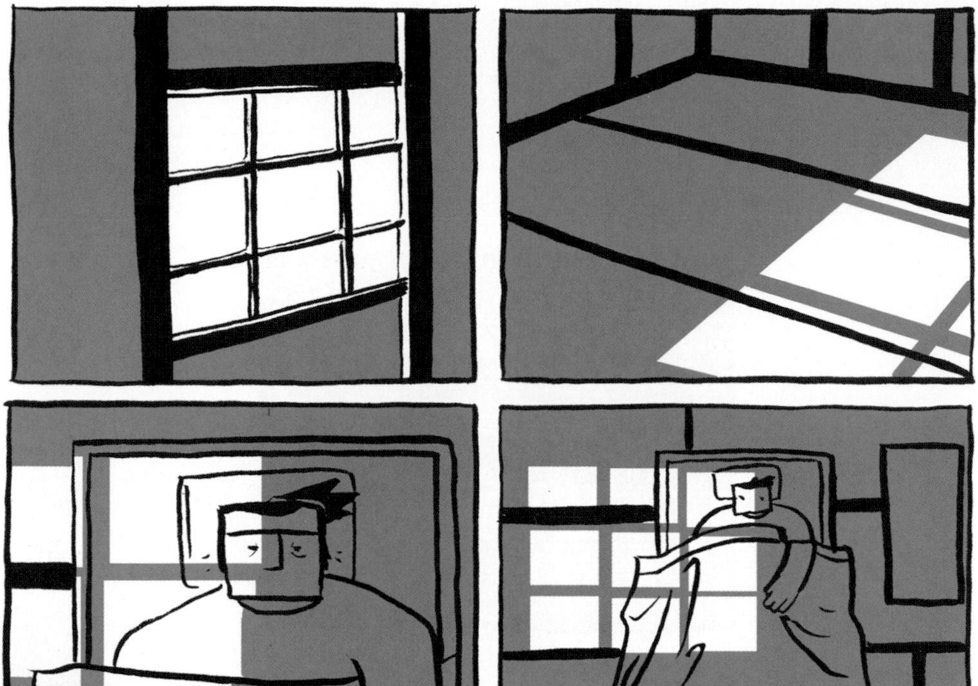
What am I doing here?

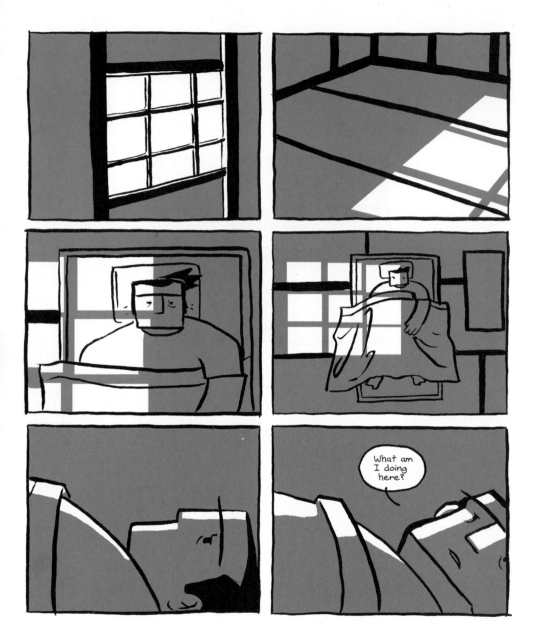

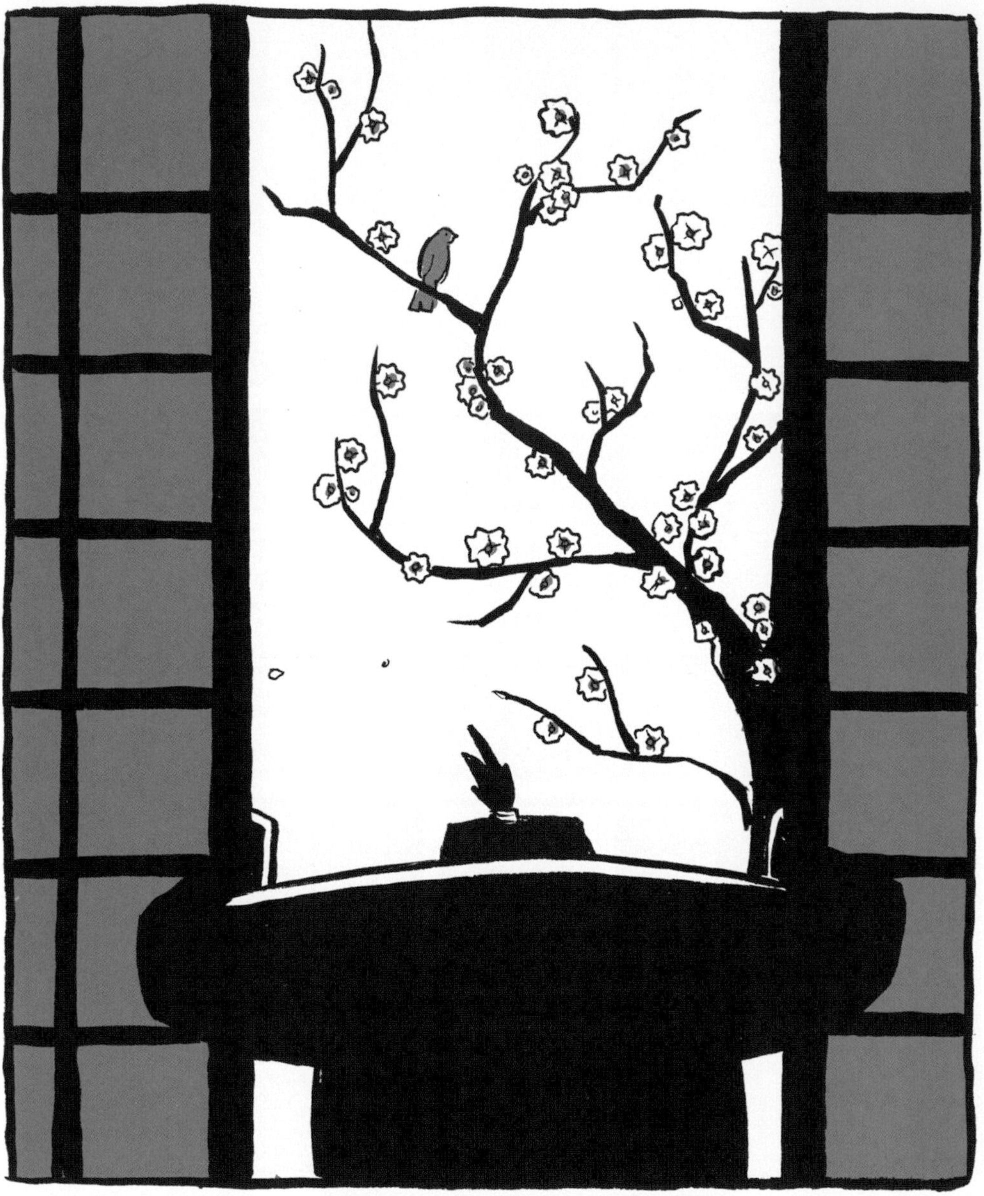

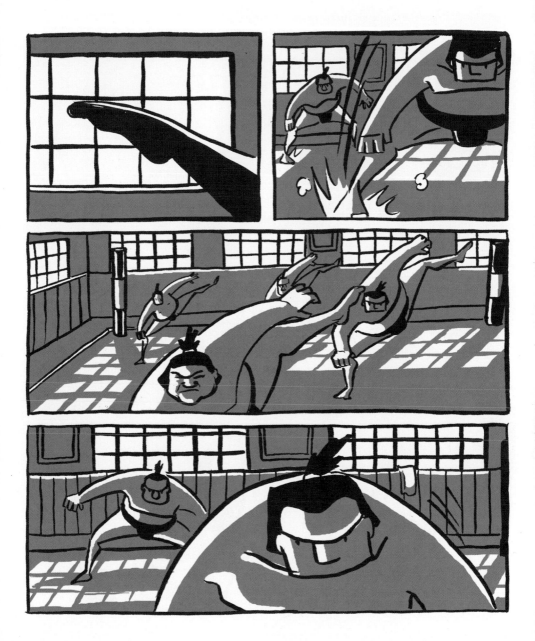

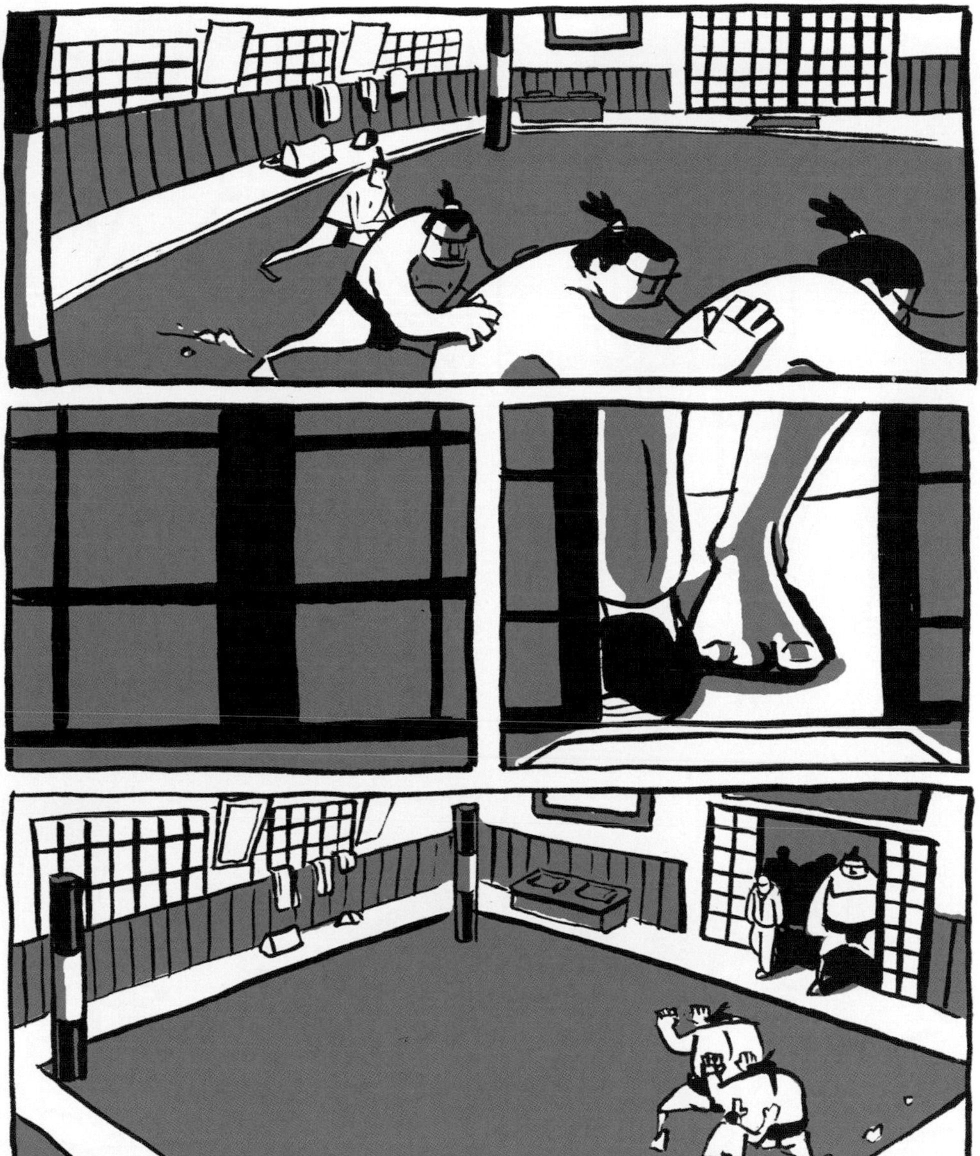

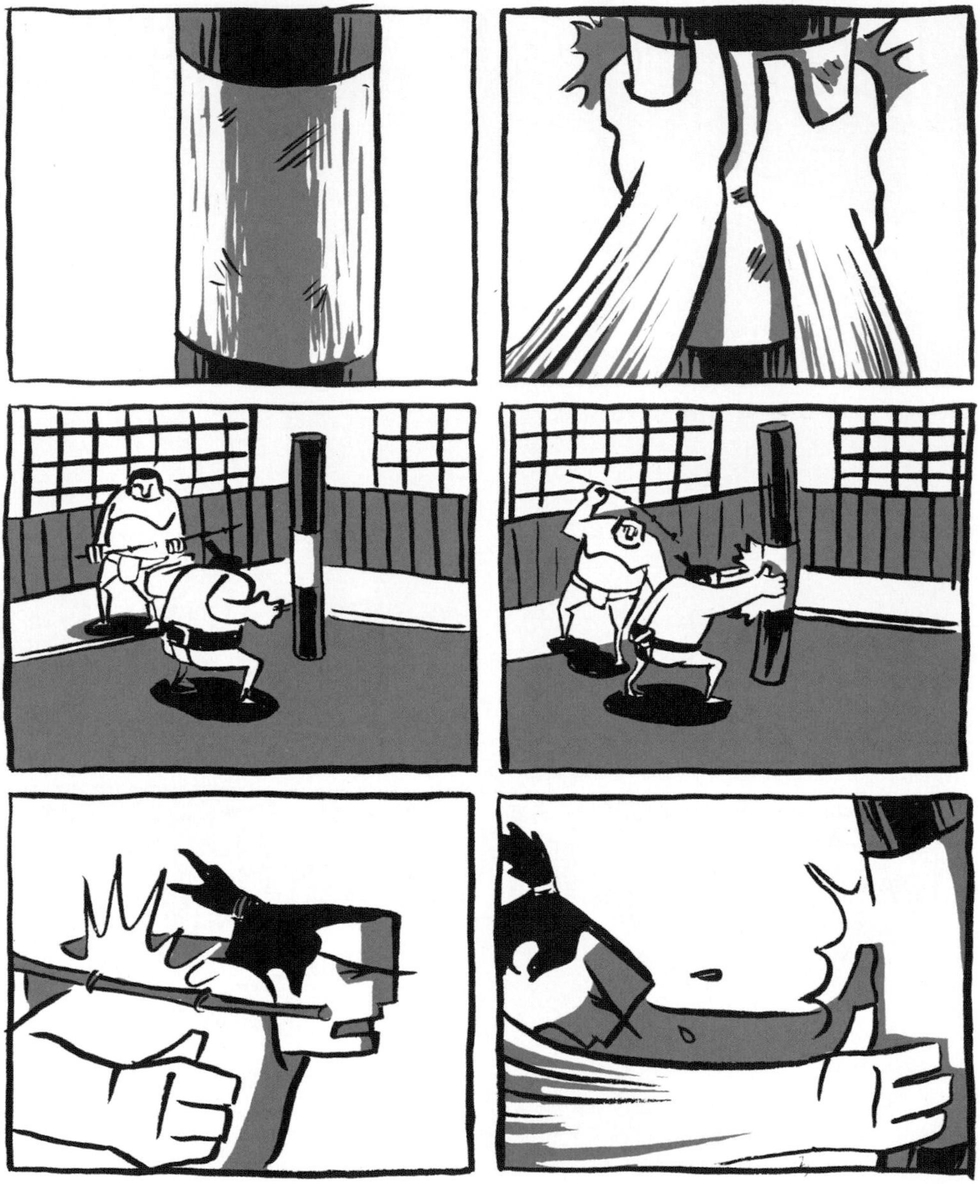

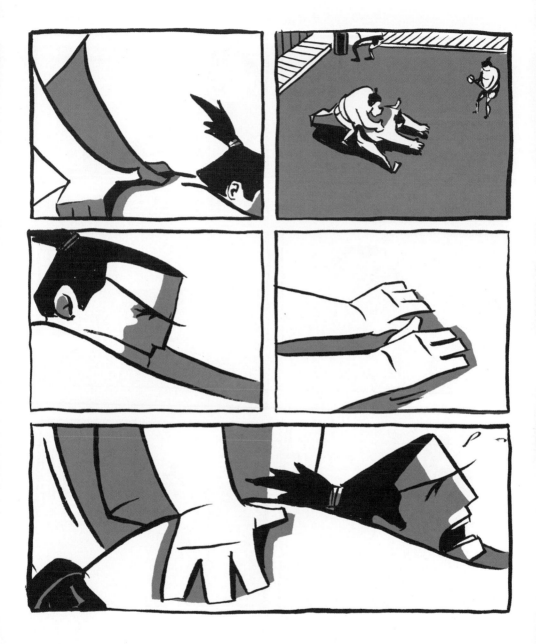

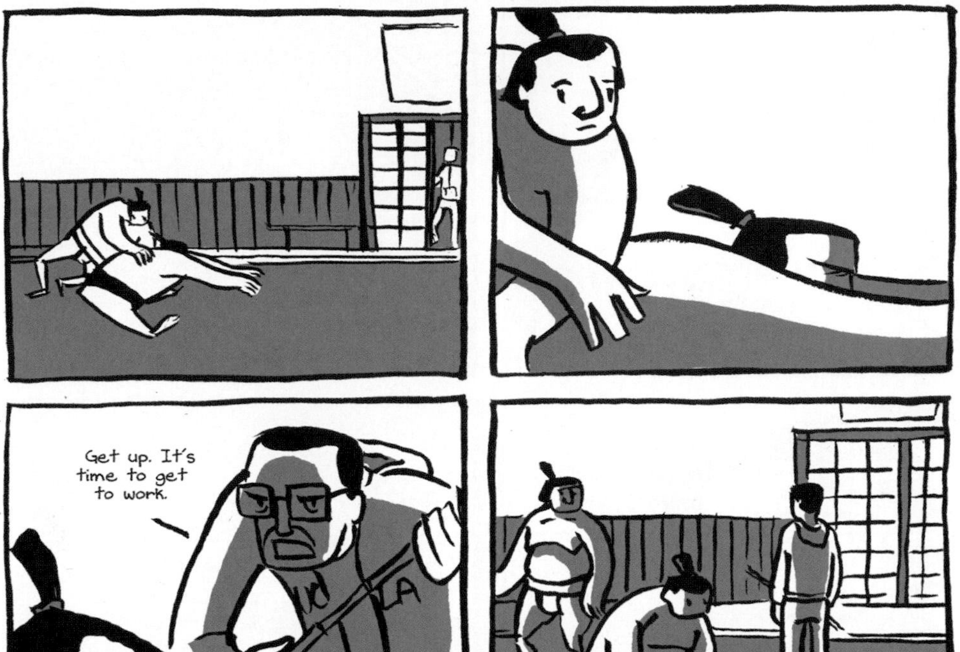
Get up. It's time to get to work.
UCLA

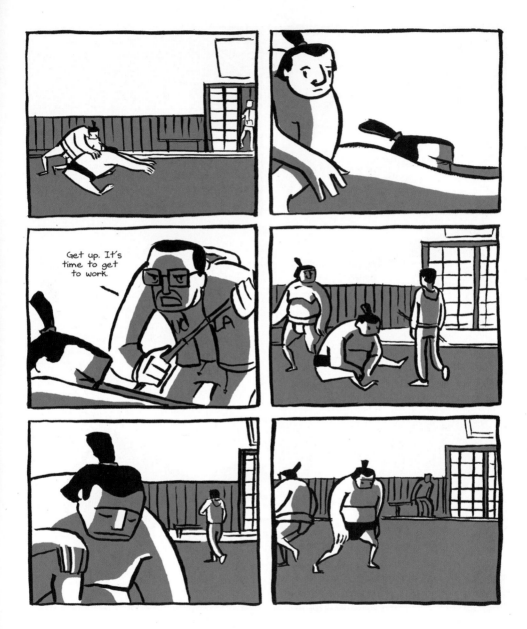

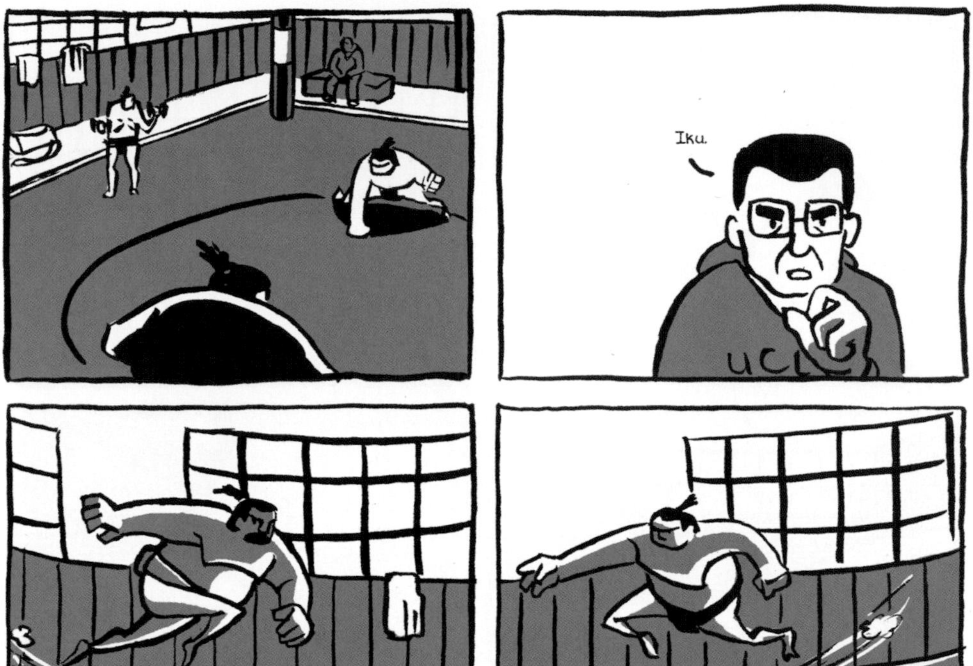
Iku.
UCL

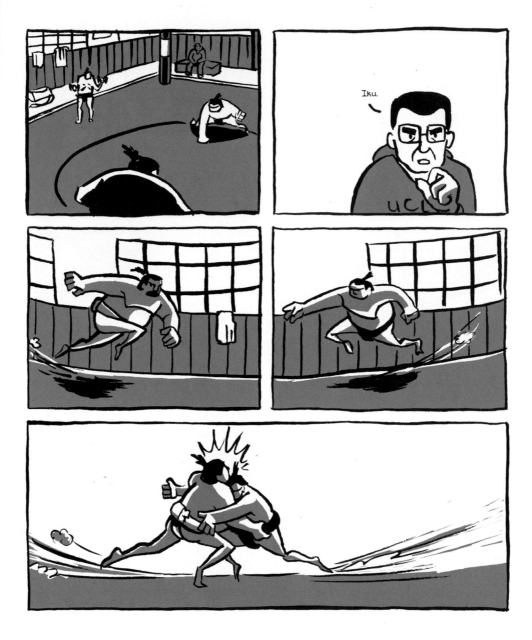

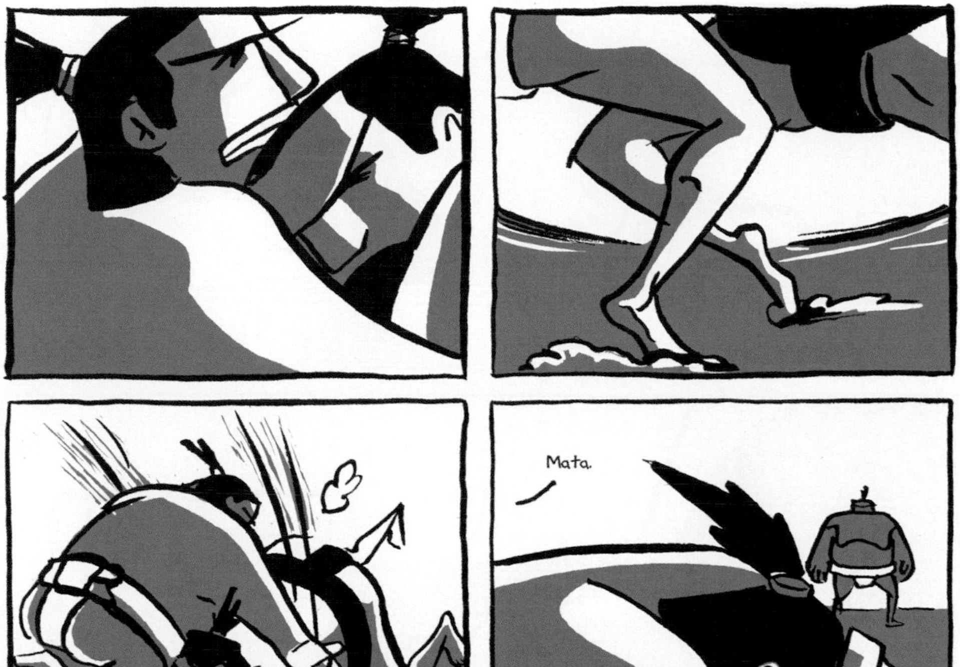
Mata.

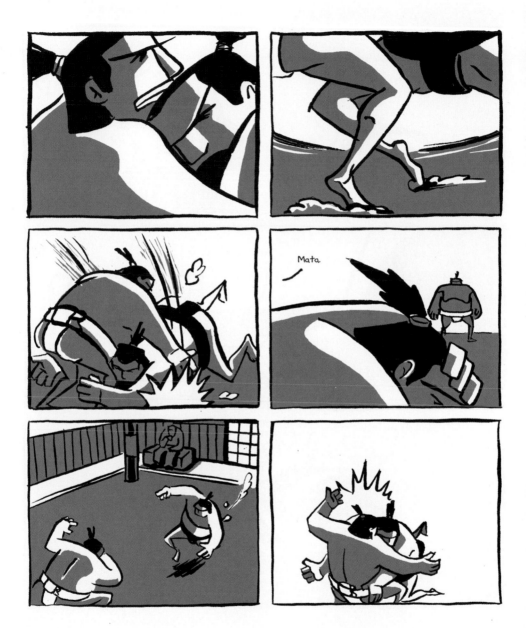

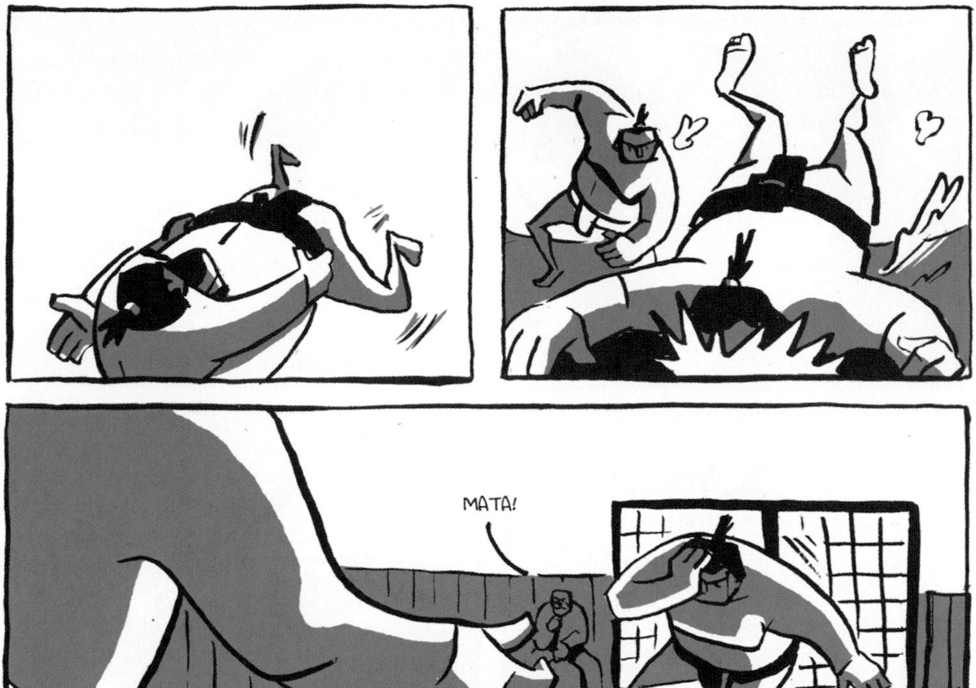
MATA!

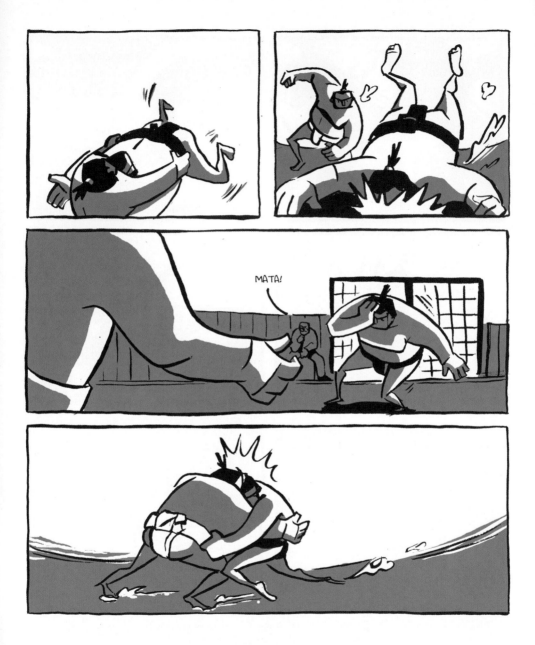

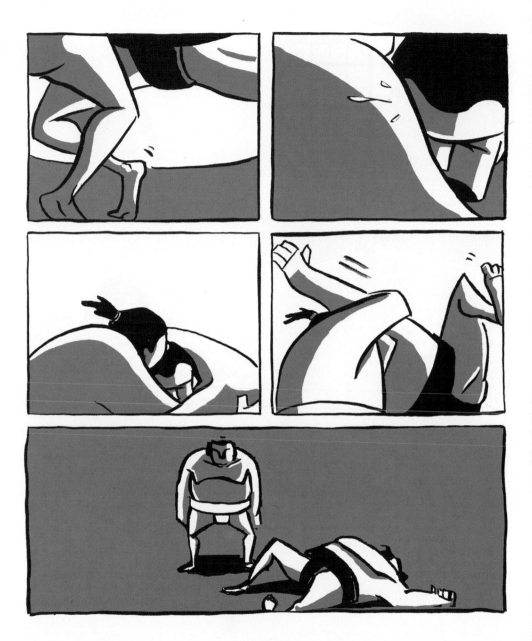

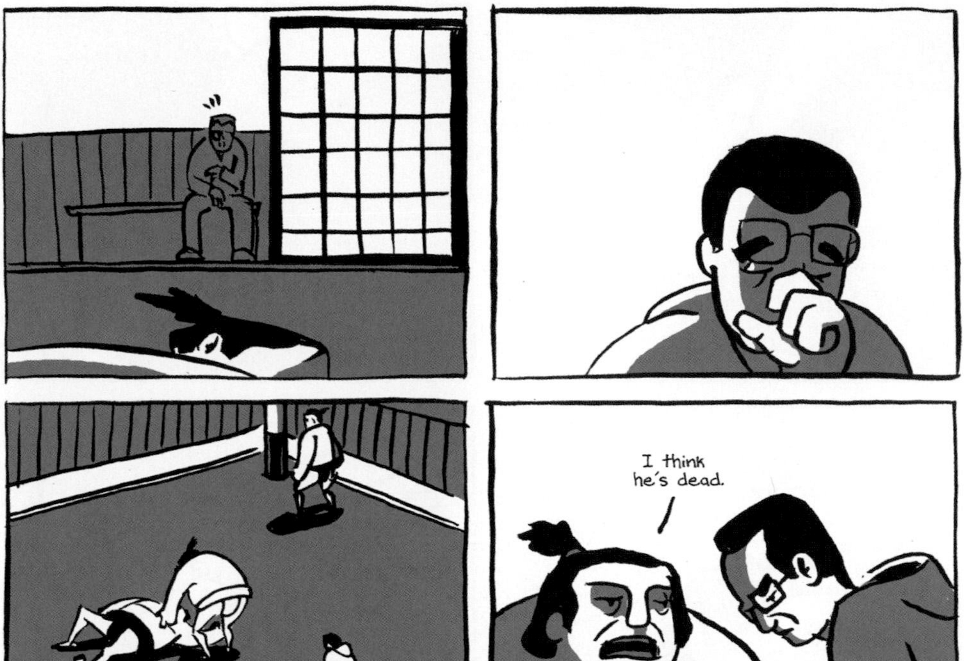
I think
he's dead.

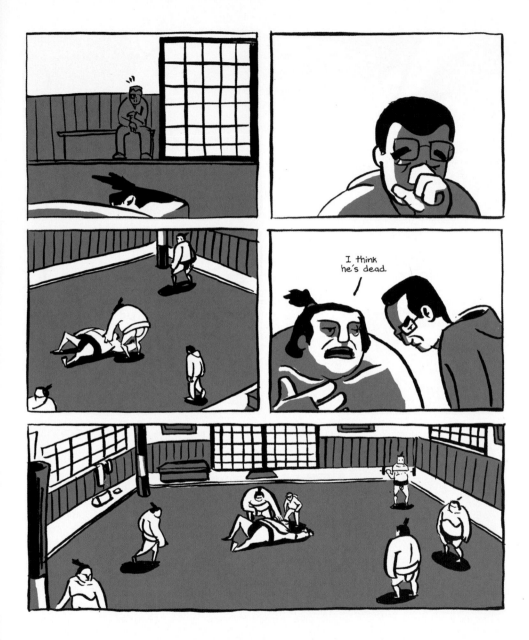

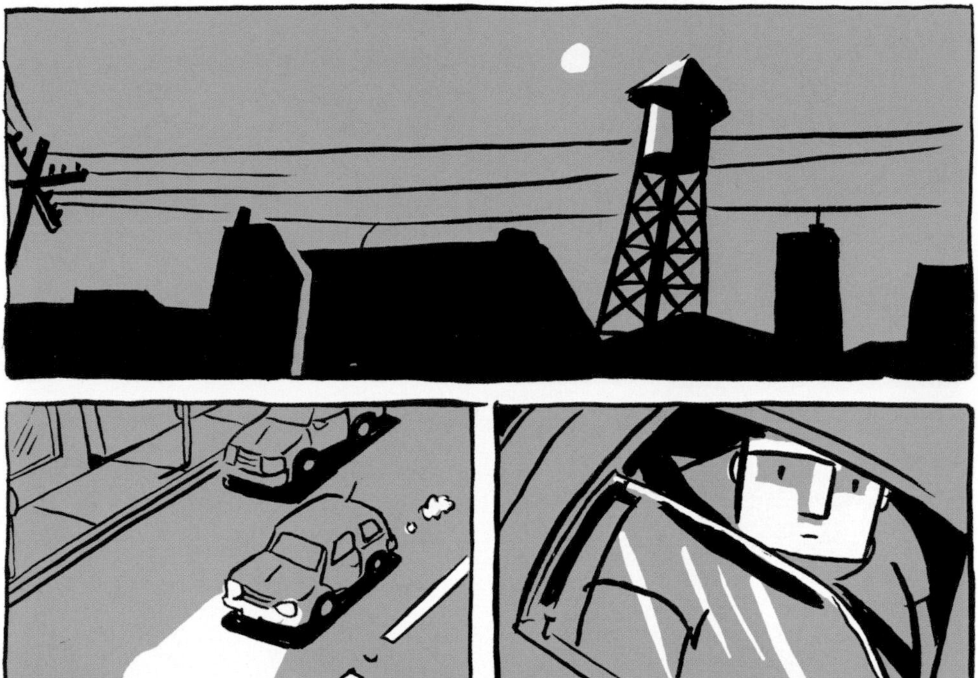
It's a nice night out.

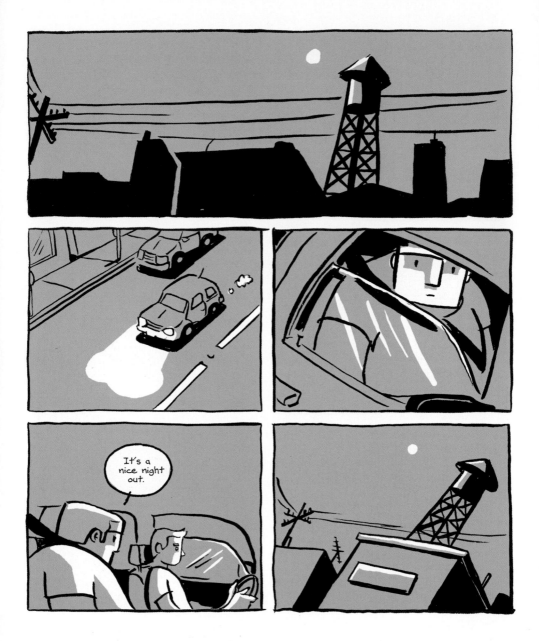

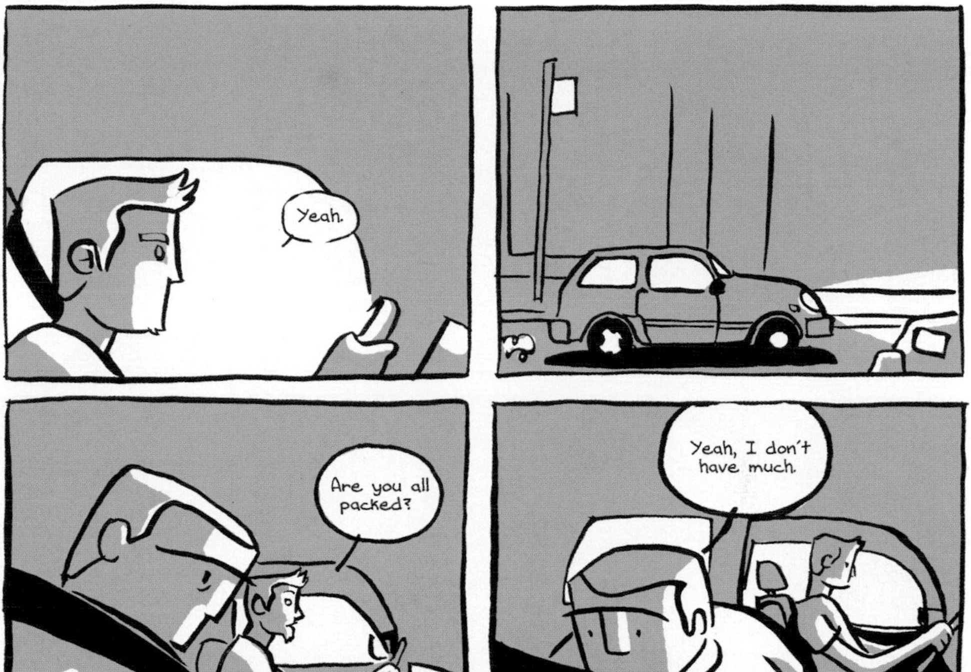
Yeah.
Are you all packed?
Yeah, I don't have much.

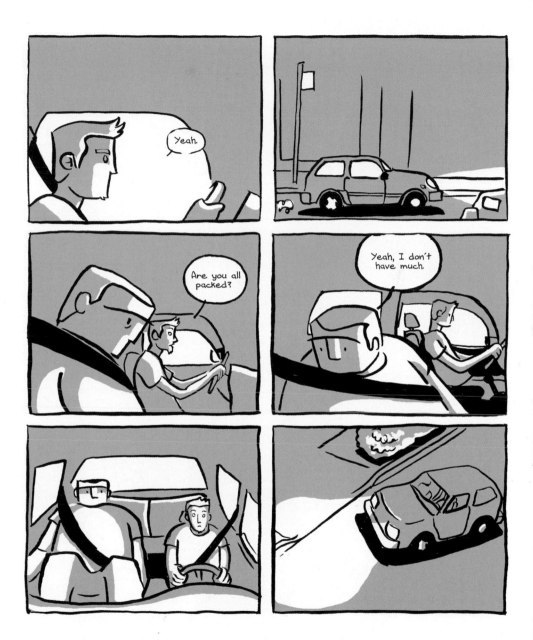

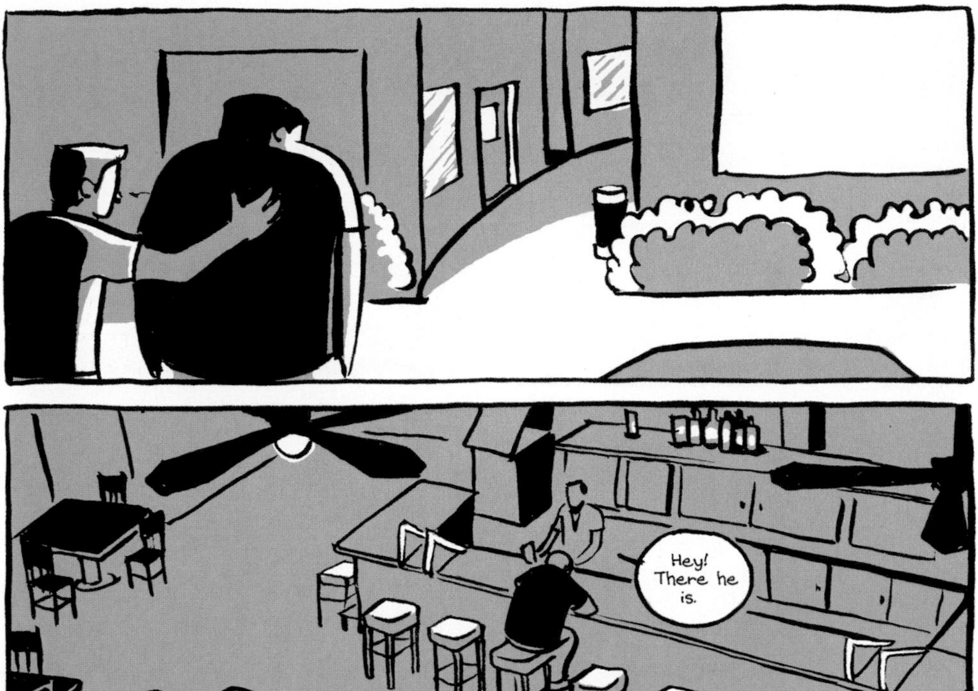
Hey! There he is.
Where's all the balloons and stuff?
This isn't Chuck E. Cheese, bro.

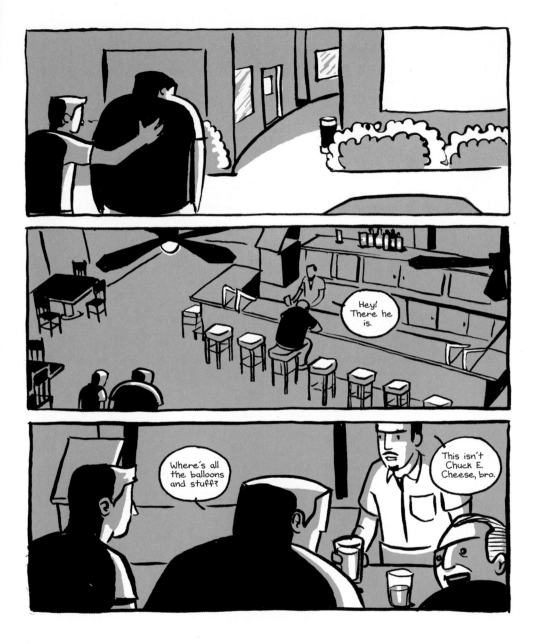

Last drink with the guys.

Dude, Japan's great. You are going to love it.

How do you know? You've never been there.

Yeah, well still...

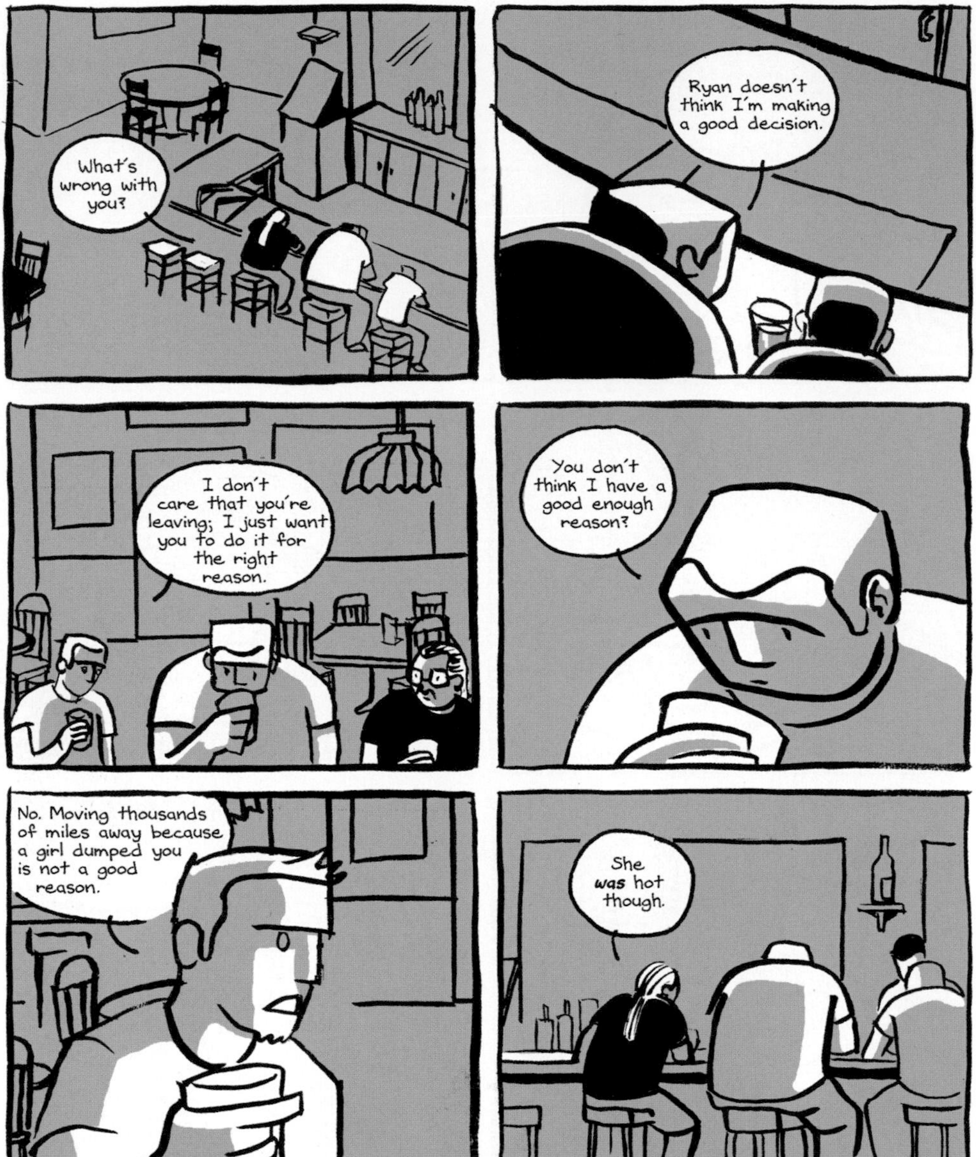
What's wrong with you?
Ryan doesn't think I'm making a good decision.
I don't care that you're leaving; I just want you to do it for the right reason.
You don't think I have a good enough reason?
No. Moving thousands of miles away because a girl dumped you is not a good reason.
She **was** hot though.

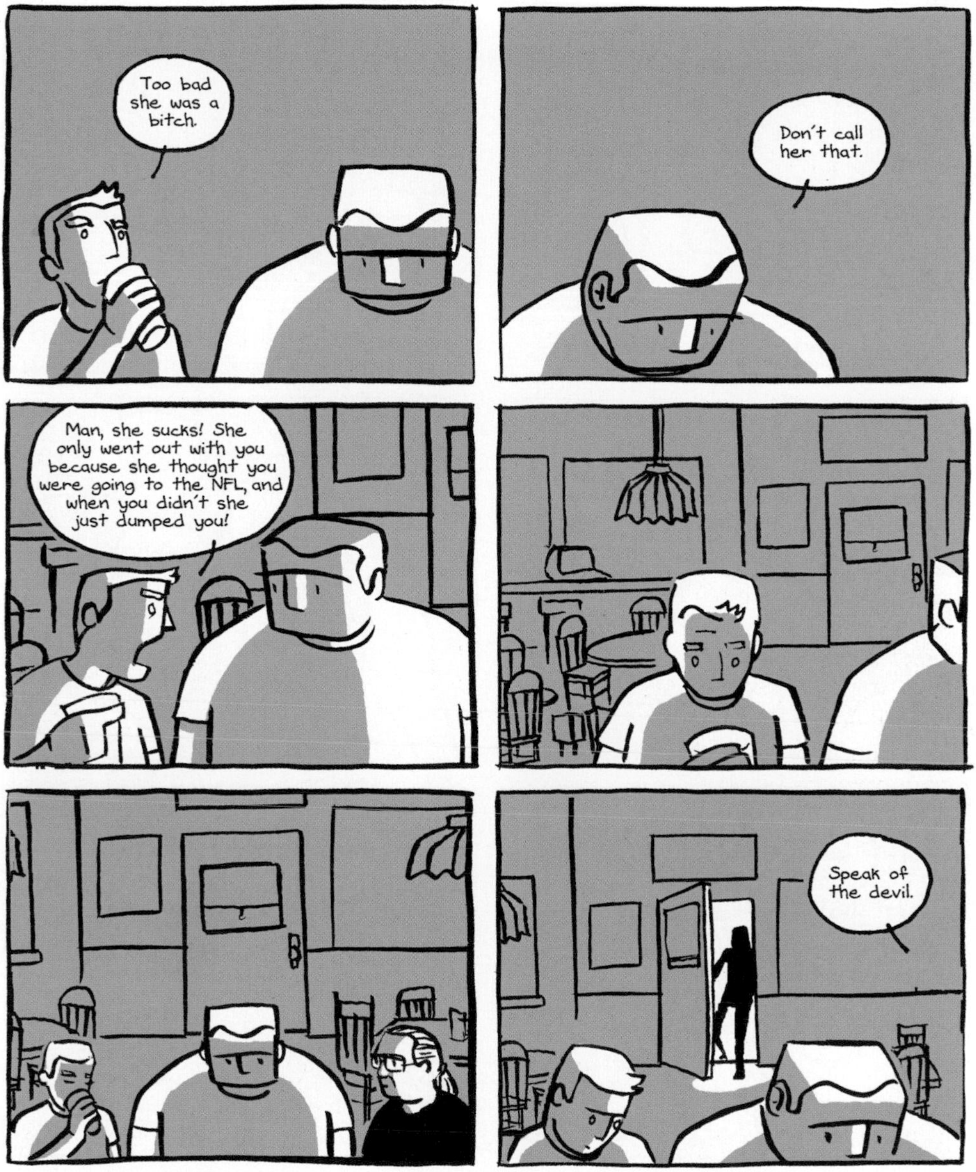
Too bad she was a bitch.
Don't call her that.
Man, she sucks! She only went out with you because she thought you were going to the NFL, and when you didn't she just dumped you!
Speak of the devil.

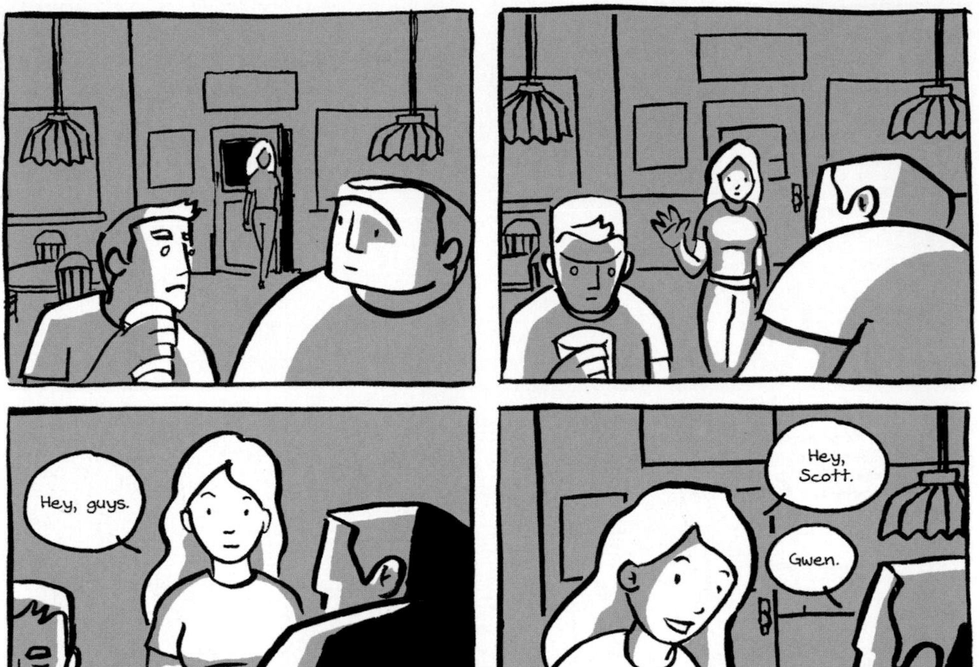
Hey, guys.
Hey, Scott.
Gwen.
What are you doing here?
Well, I wasn't going to let you leave without saying goodbye.
Gwen, you want a drink? Evans is buying.
Wwwhat?

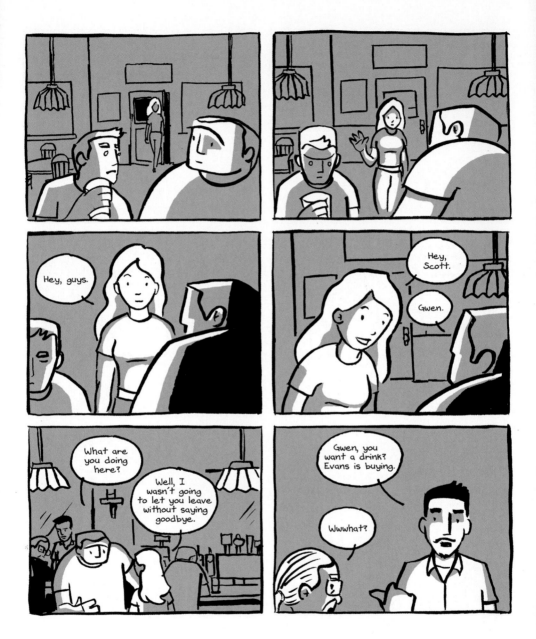

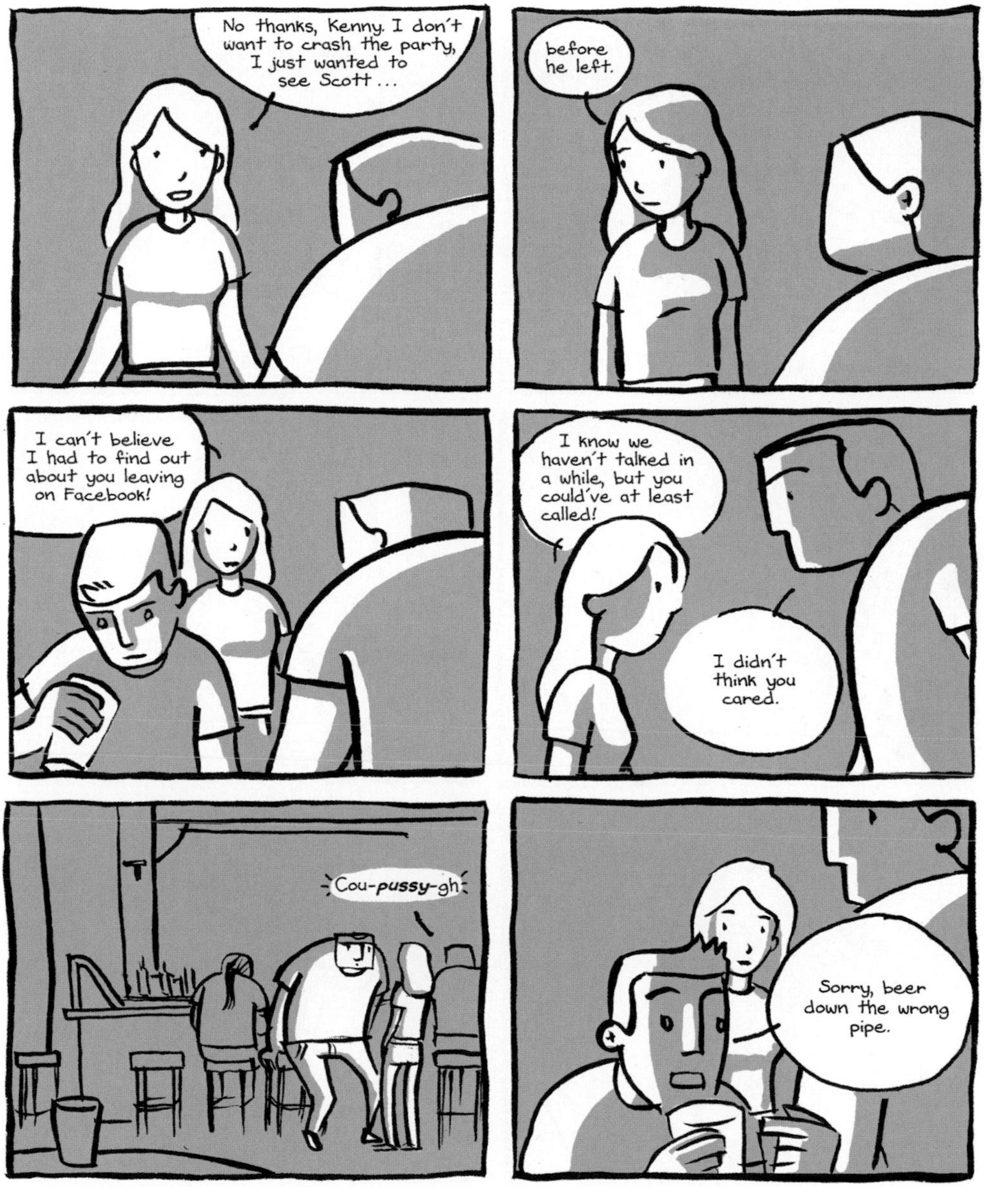
No thanks, Kenny. I don't want to crash the party, I just wanted to see Scott . . .
before he left.
I can't believe I had to find out about you leaving on Facebook!
I know we haven't talked in a while, but you could've at least called!
I didn't think you cared.
Cou-pussy-gh
Sorry, beer down the wrong pipe.

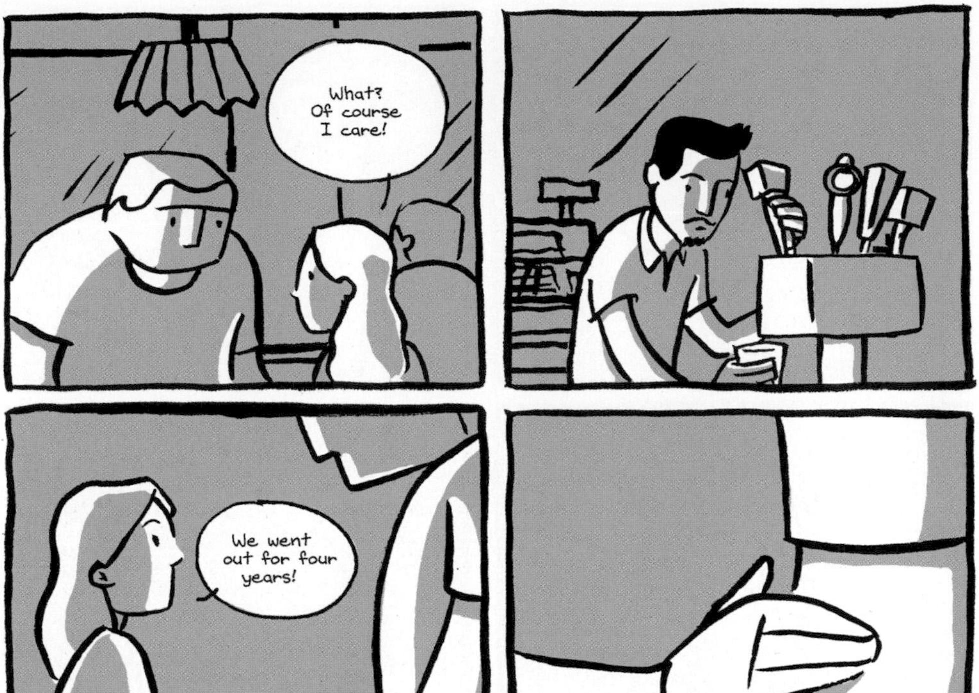

What? Of course I care!
We went out for four years!
Can we talk before you leave?
Call me when you get home tonight, okay?

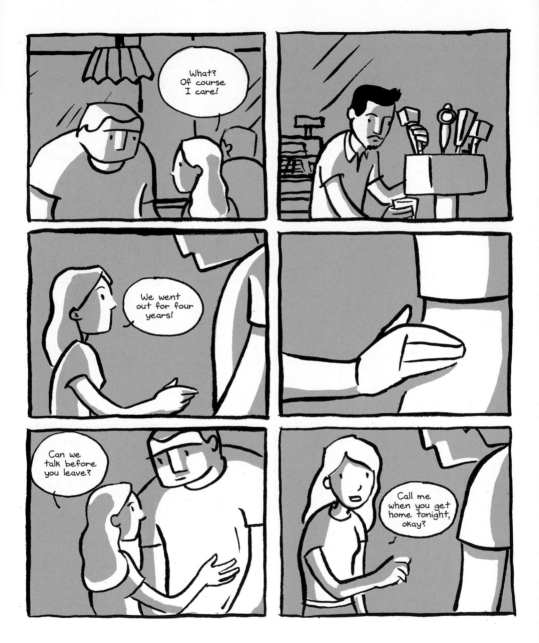

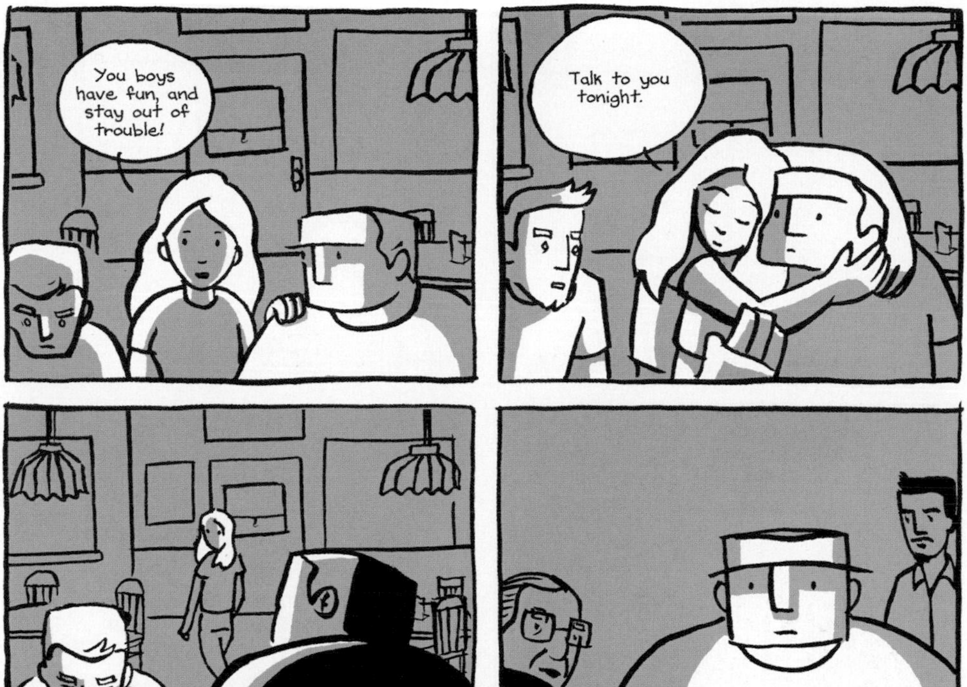
You boys have fun, and stay out of trouble!
Talk to you tonight.

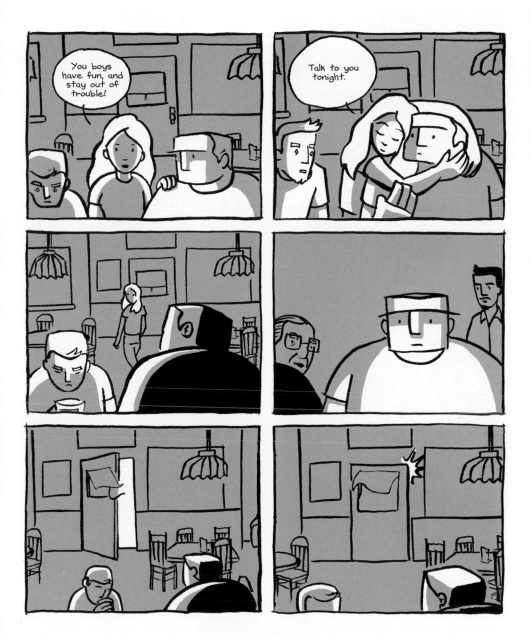

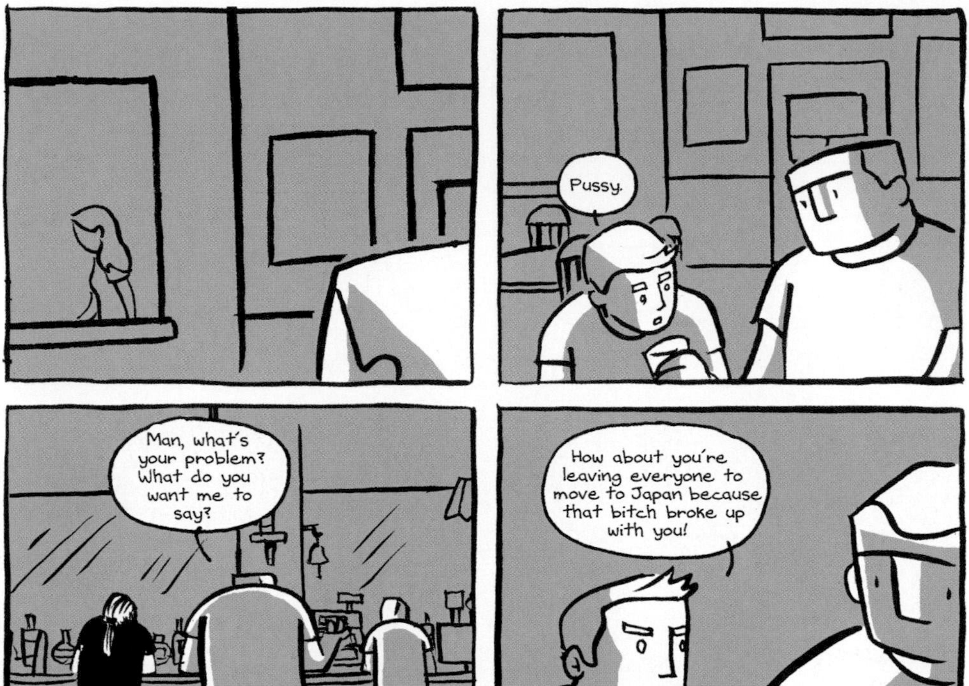
Pussy.
Man, what's your problem? What do you want me to say?
How about you're leaving everyone to move to Japan because that bitch broke up with you!
I think you'll do great in Japan.

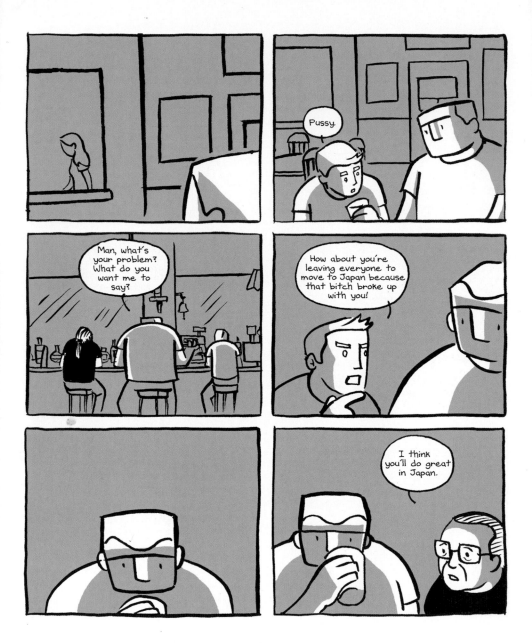

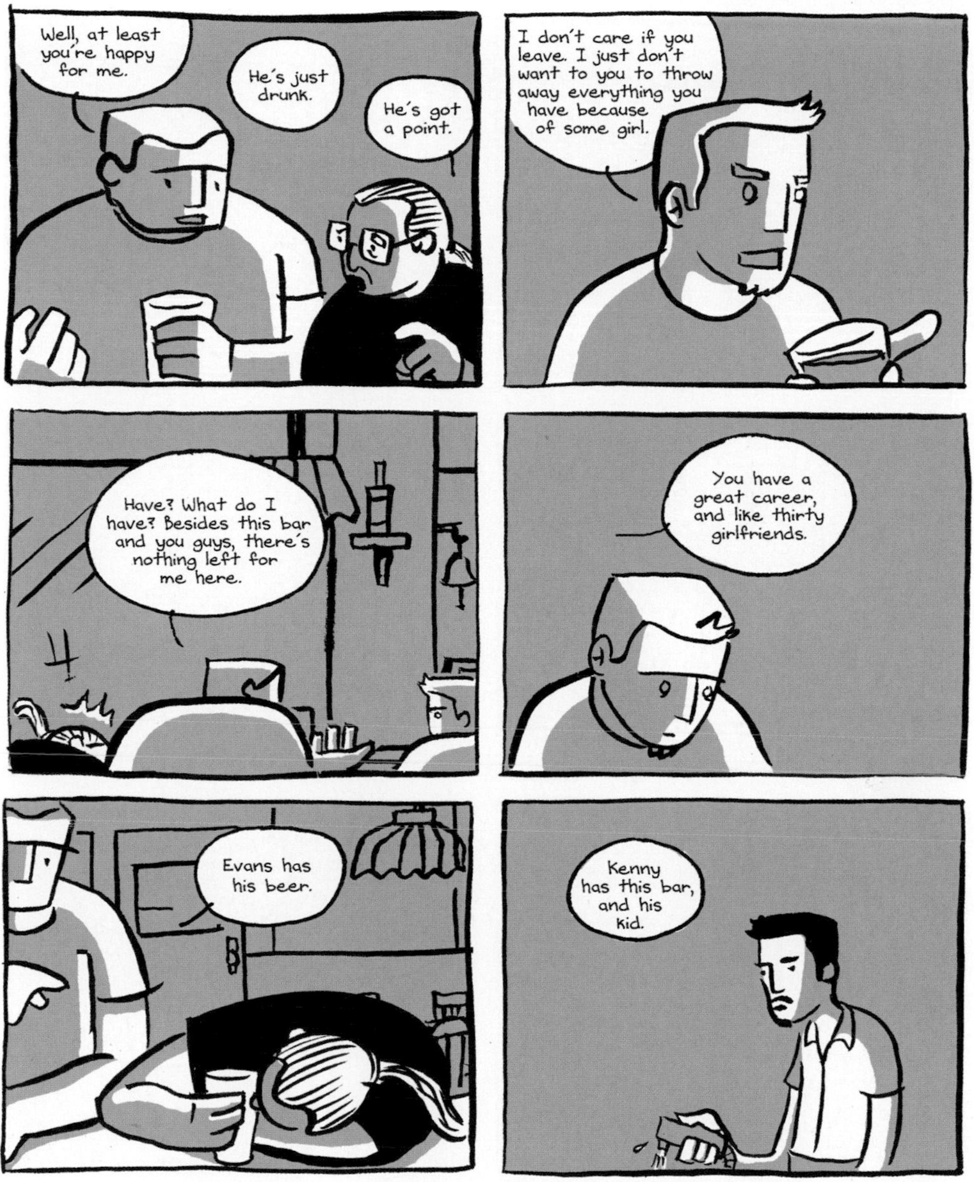
Well, at least you're happy for me.
He's just drunk.
He's got a point.
I don't care if you leave. I just don't want to you to throw away everything you have because of some girl.
Have? What do I have? Besides this bar and you guys, there's nothing left for me here.
You have a great career, and like thirty girlfriends.
Evans has his beer.
Kenny has this bar, and his kid.

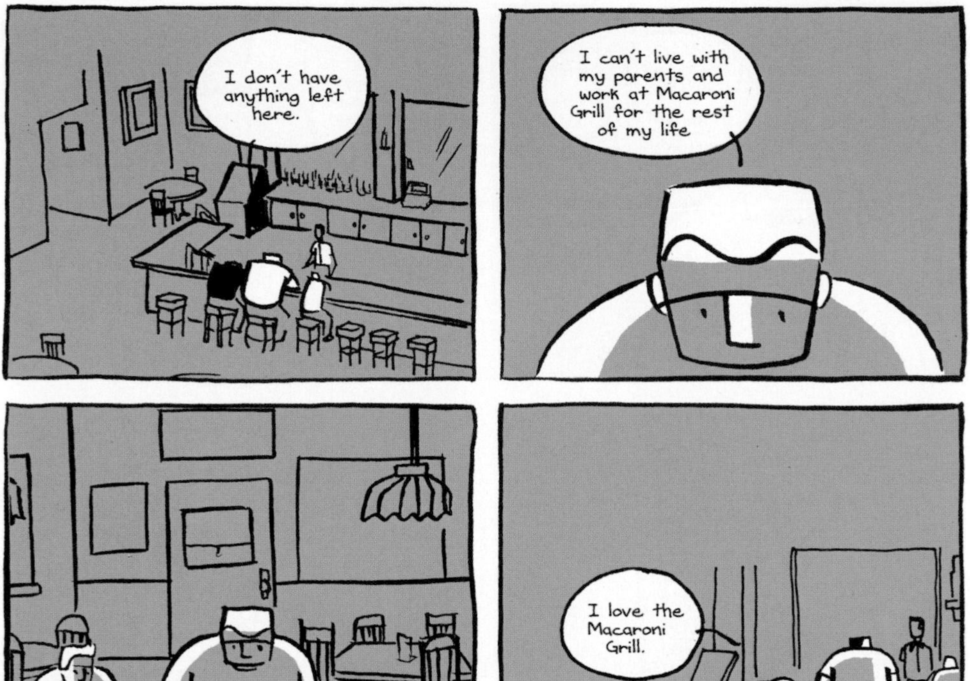
I don't have anything left here.
I can't live with my parents and work at Macaroni Grill for the rest of my life
I love the Macaroni Grill.
Man, what's wrong with you guys? This is supposed to be a party.
Here's to our boy, may he get insanely fat, and excel at rolling around with sweaty, half-naked men!

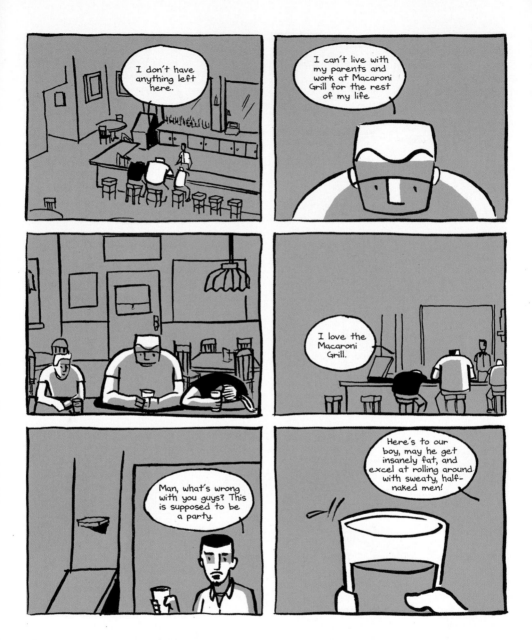

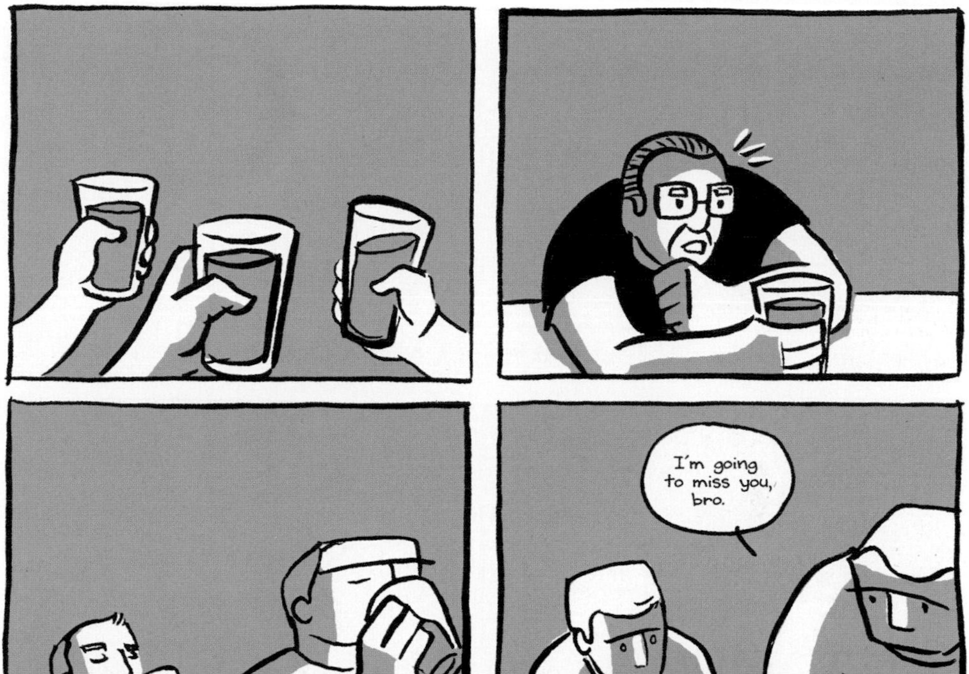
I'm going to miss you, bro.
What am I going to do without my best bro?
Pussy.

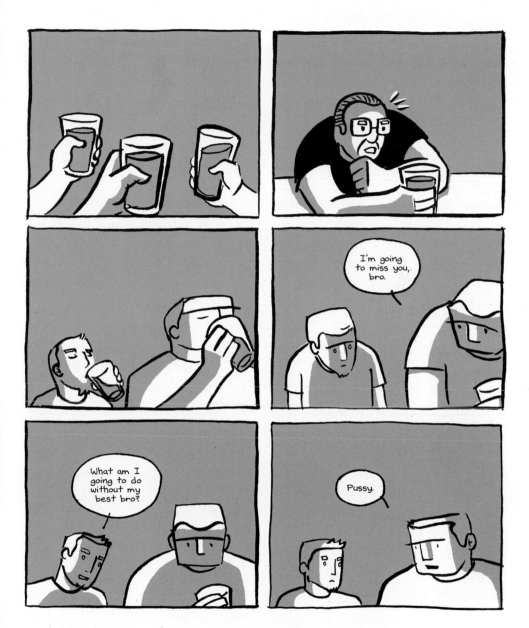

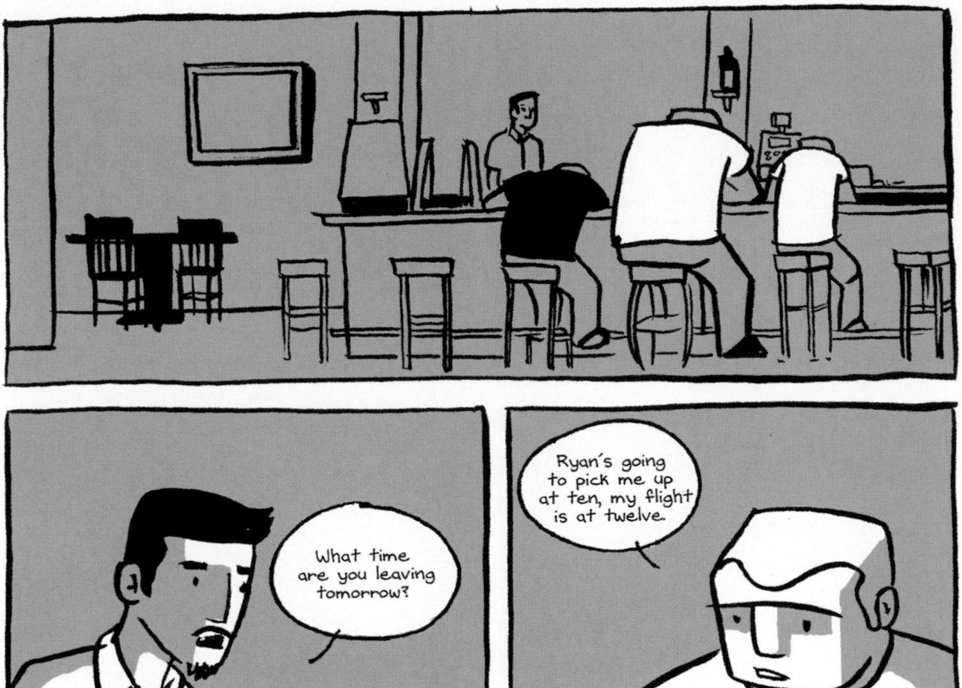
What time are you leaving tomorrow?
Ryan´s going to pick me up at ten, my flight is at twelve.

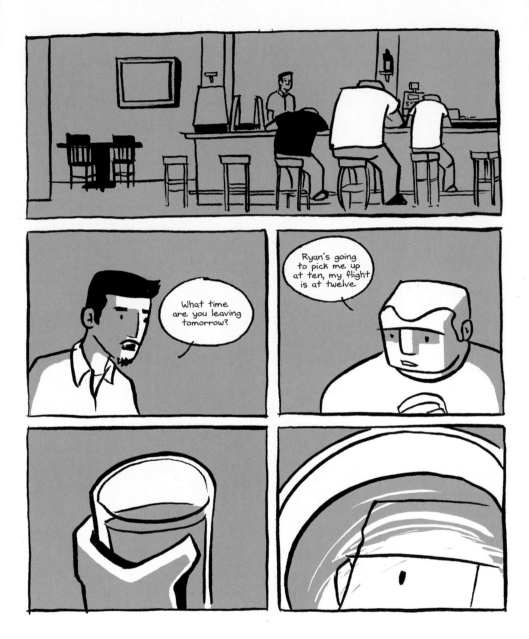

You are disgracing my dojo! Get up and go do your chores.

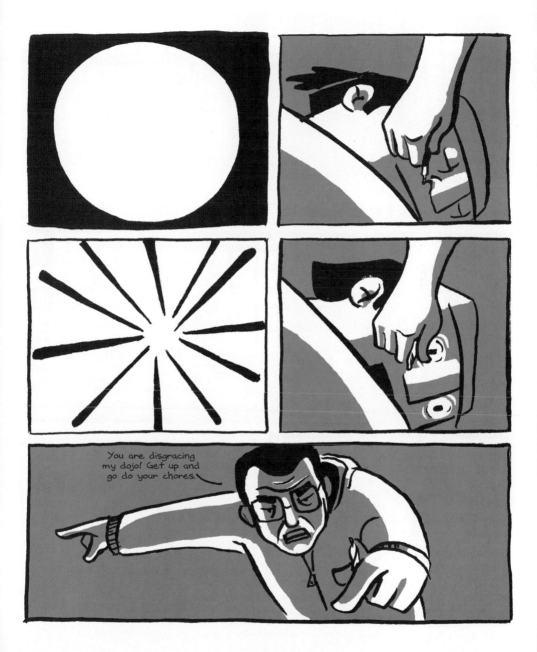

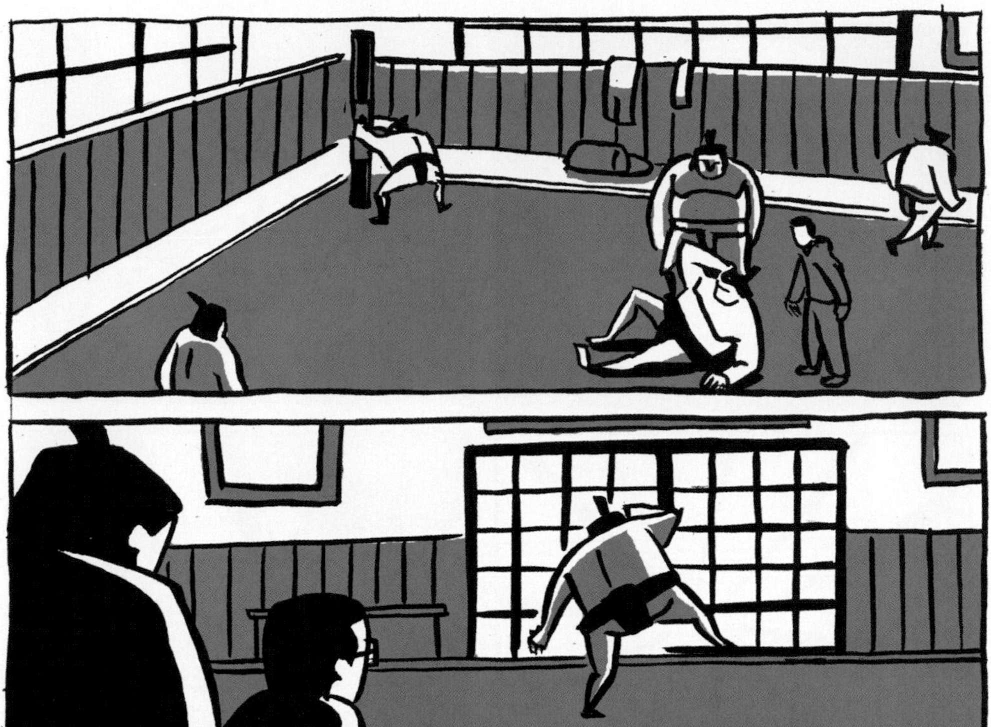
Do you think he'll make it?
I don't know...
UCLA
I hope so.

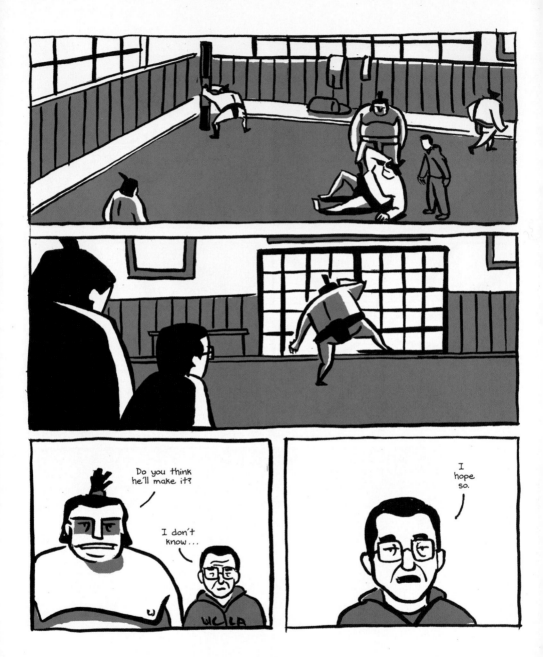

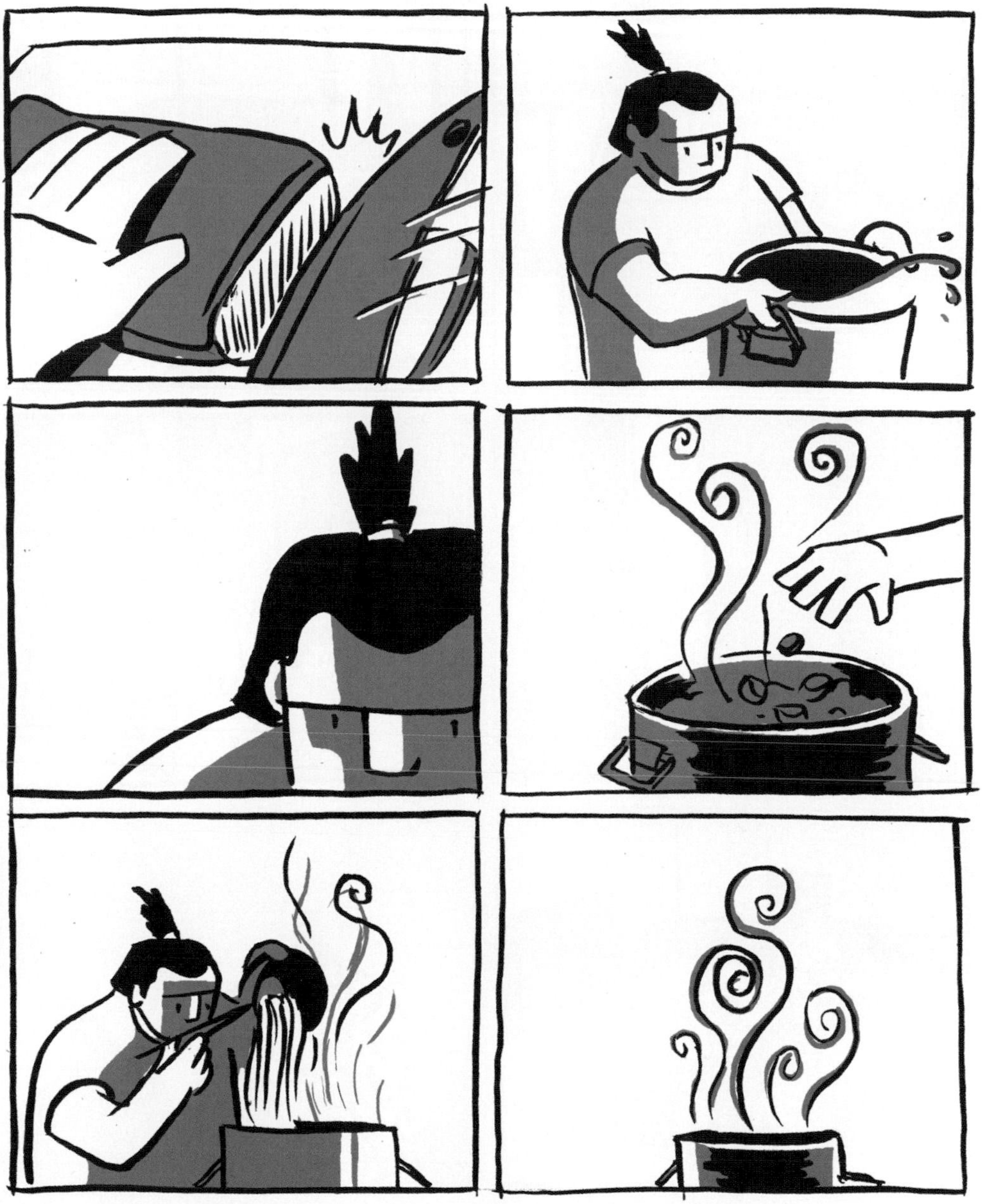

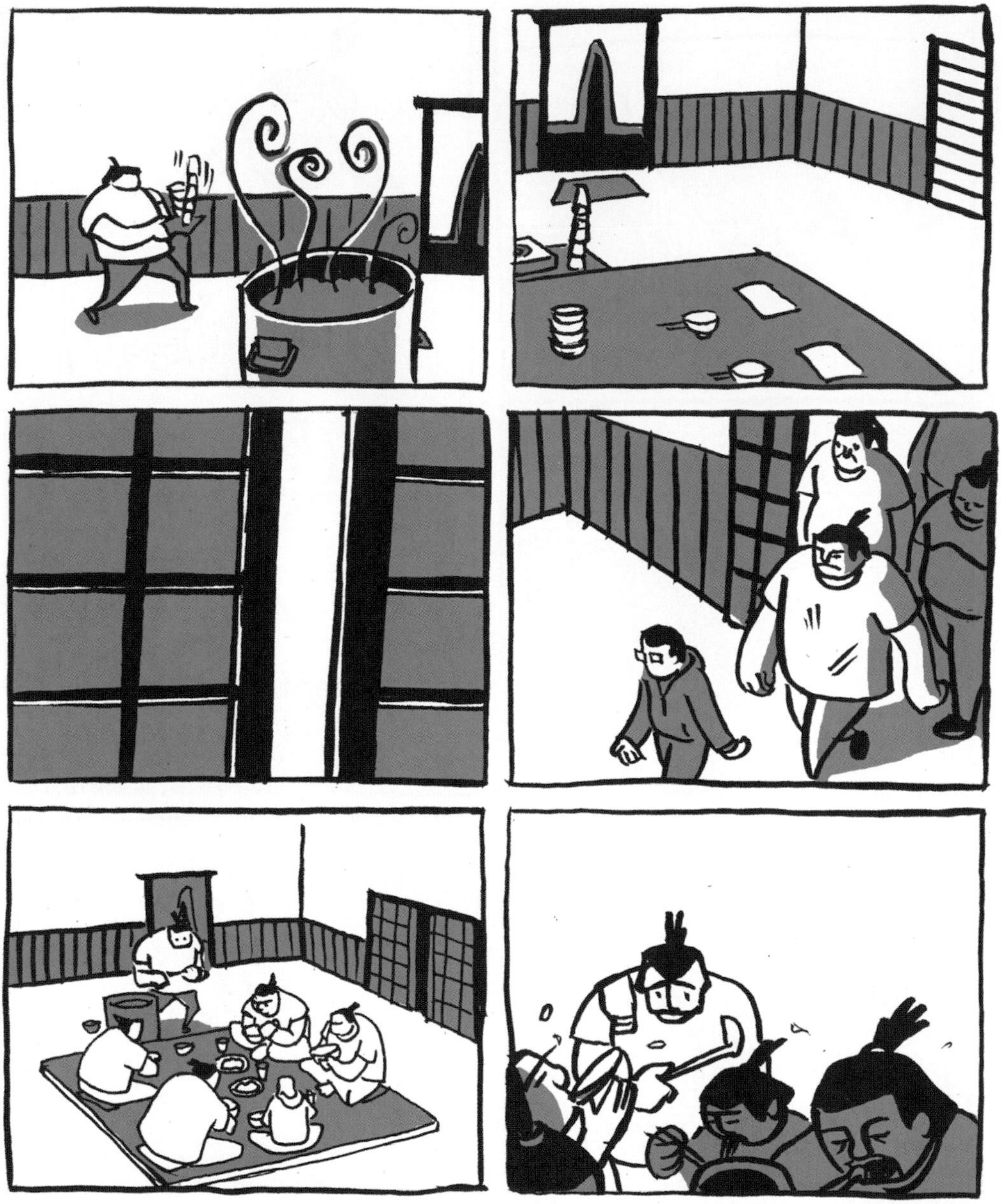

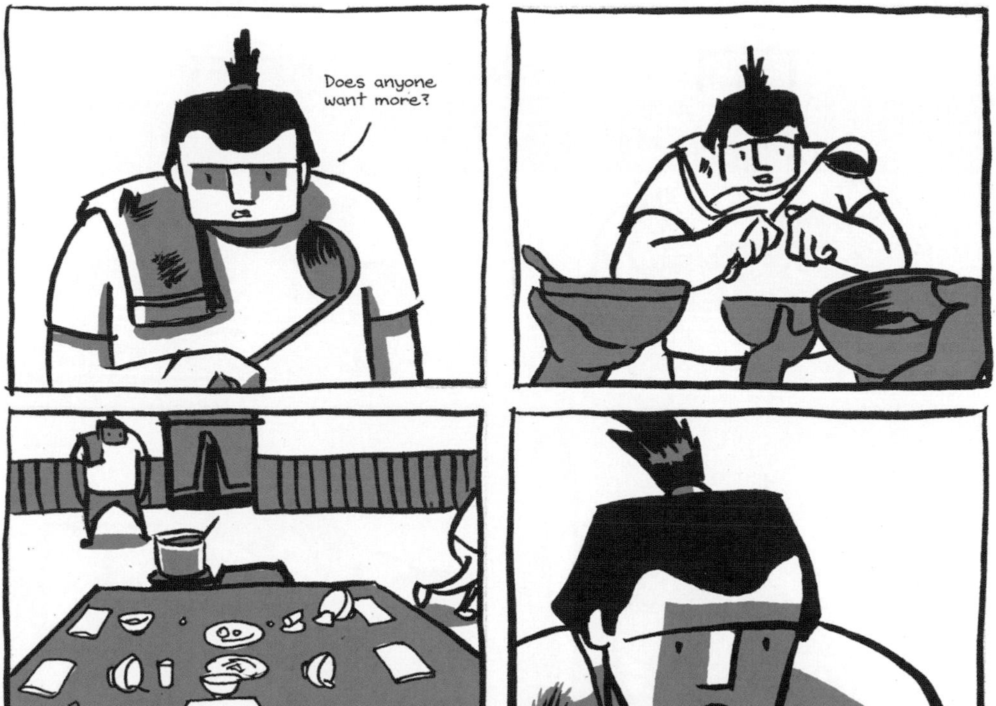
Does anyone want more?
I hope those guys didn't eat too much, because we are hungry.

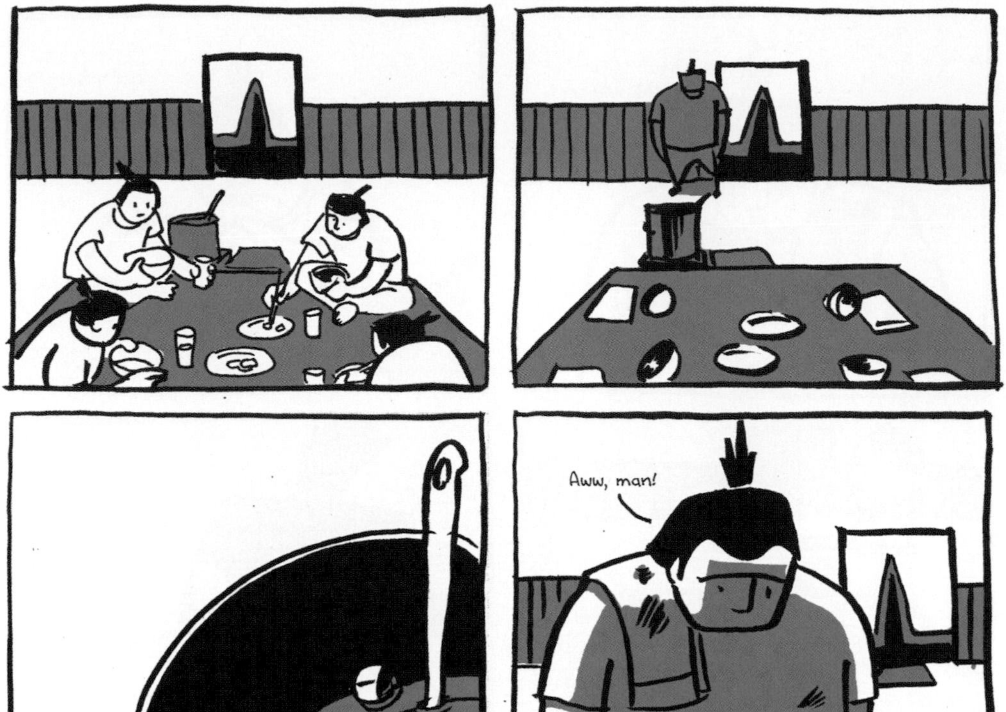
Aww, man!
Asami. What? Why aren't you eating with your mom?
I heard you were cooking today, and you know how much I like your nabe.

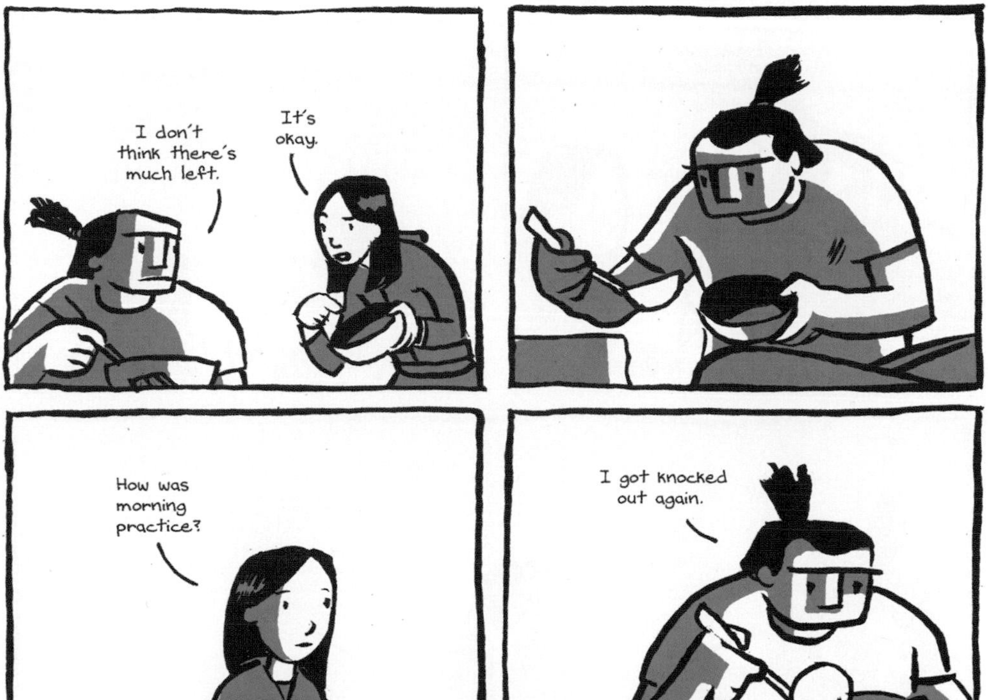
I don't think there's much left.
It's okay.
How was morning practice?
I got knocked out again.
Here.
Is this all that's left?

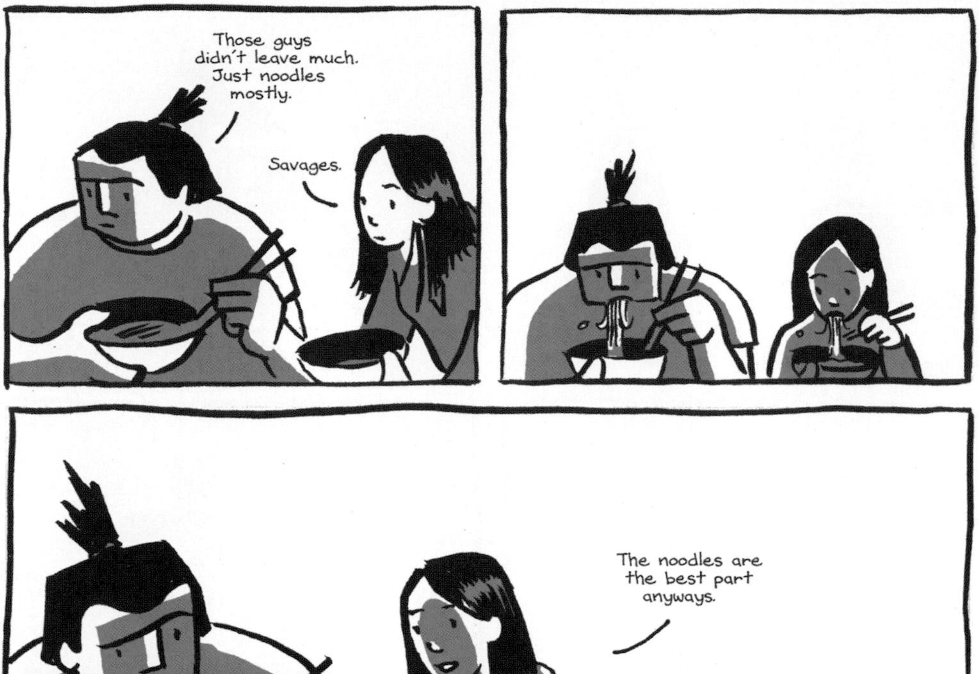
Those guys didn't leave much. Just noodles mostly.
Savages.
The noodles are the best part anyways.

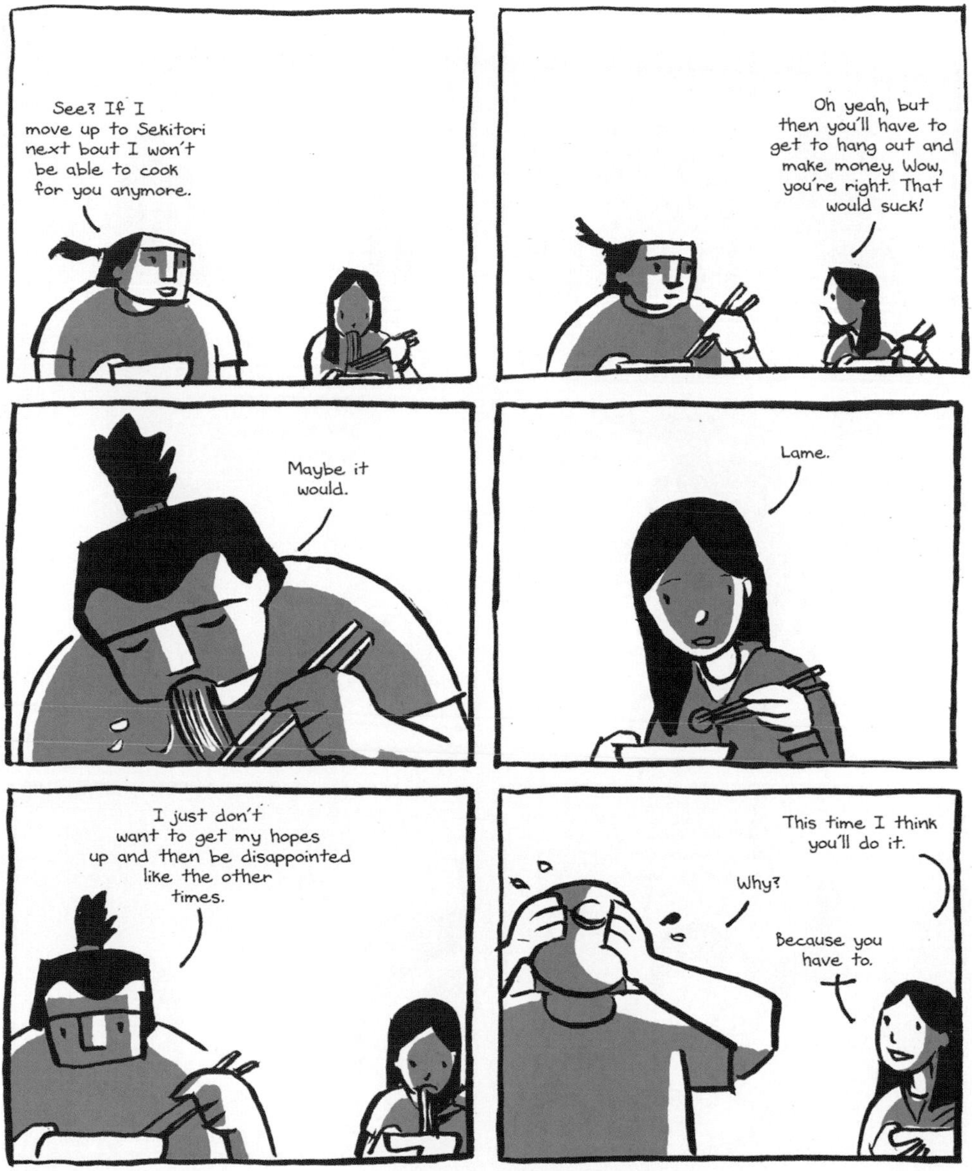
See? If I move up to Sekitori next bout I won't be able to cook for you anymore.
Oh yeah, but then you'll have to get to hang out and make money. Wow, you're right. That would suck!
Maybe it would.
Lame.
I just don't want to get my hopes up and then be disappointed like the other times.
This time I think you'll do it.
Why?
Because you have to.

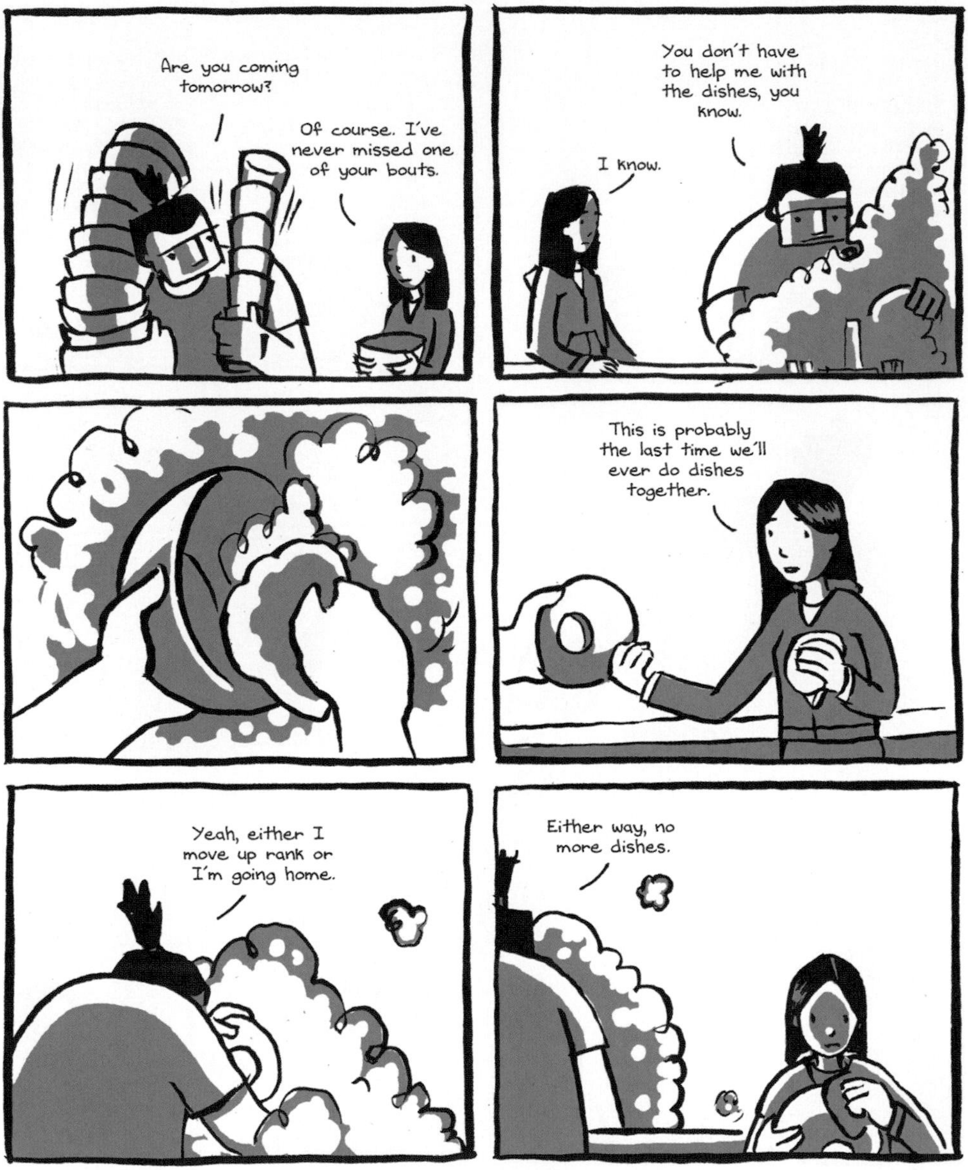

Are you coming tomorrow?
Of course. I've never missed one of your bouts.
You don't have to help me with the dishes, you know.
I know.
This is probably the last time we'll ever do dishes together.
Yeah, either I move up rank or I'm going home.
Either way, no more dishes.

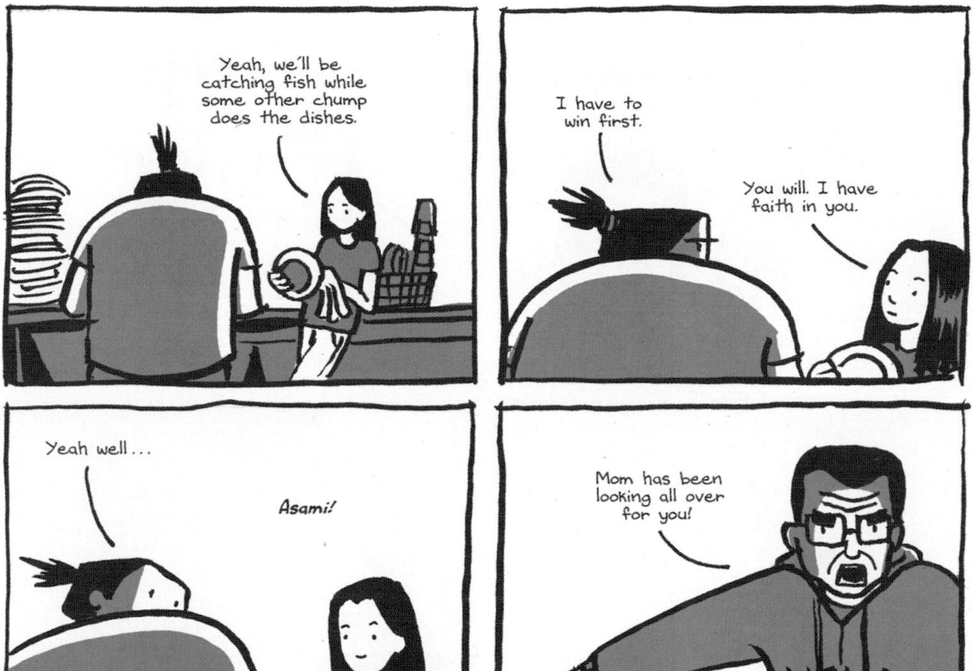
Yeah, we'll be catching fish while some other chump does the dishes.
I have to win first.
You will. I have faith in you.
Yeah well...
Asami!
Mom has been looking all over for you!
UCLA
Okay, okay. Bye.
UCLA

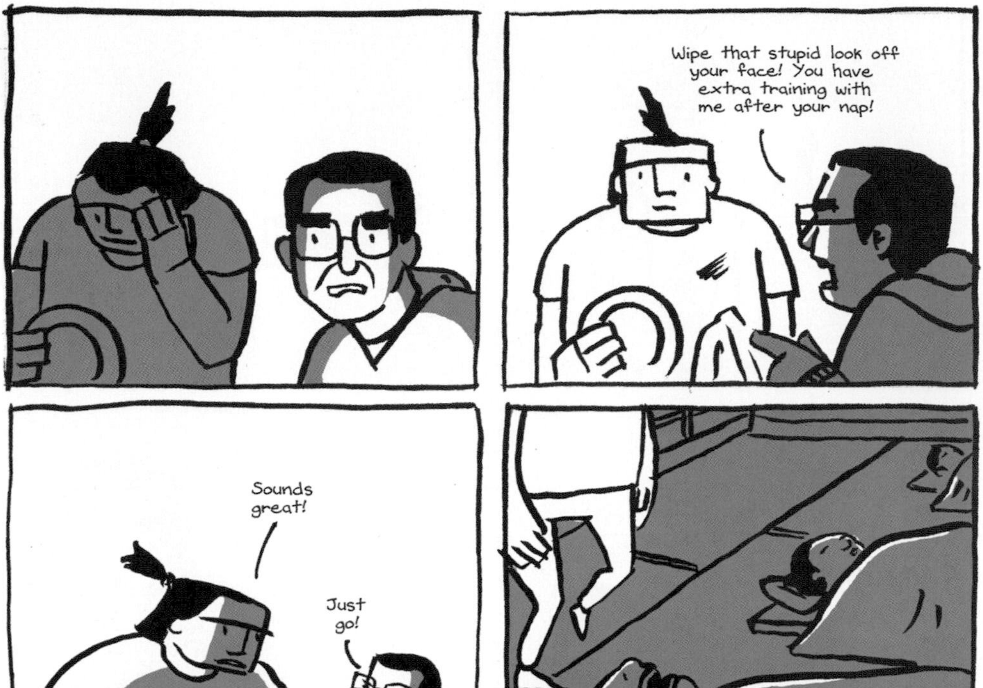
Wipe that stupid look off your face! You have extra training with me after your nap!
Sounds great!
Just go!

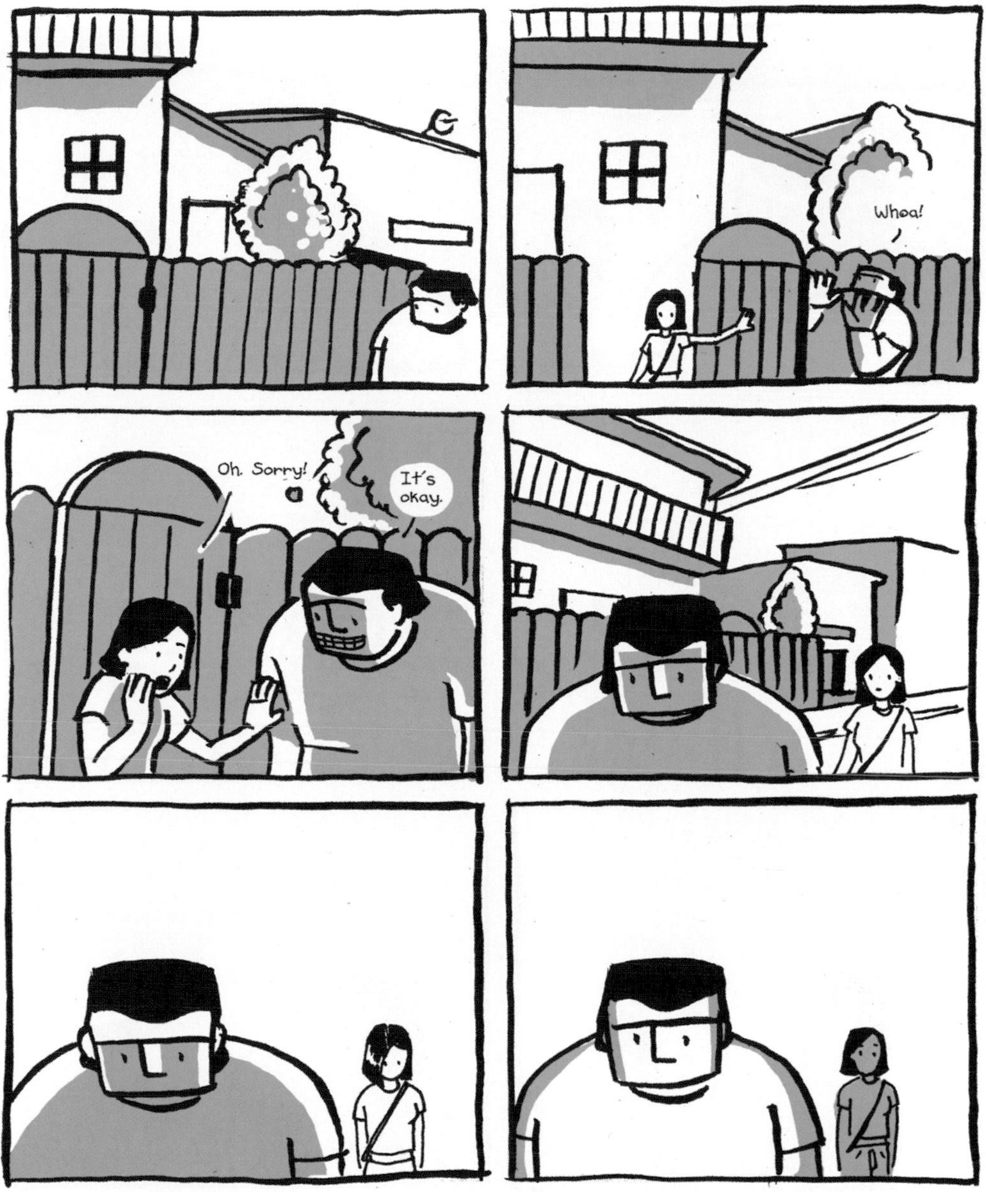
Whoa!
Oh. Sorry!
It's okay.

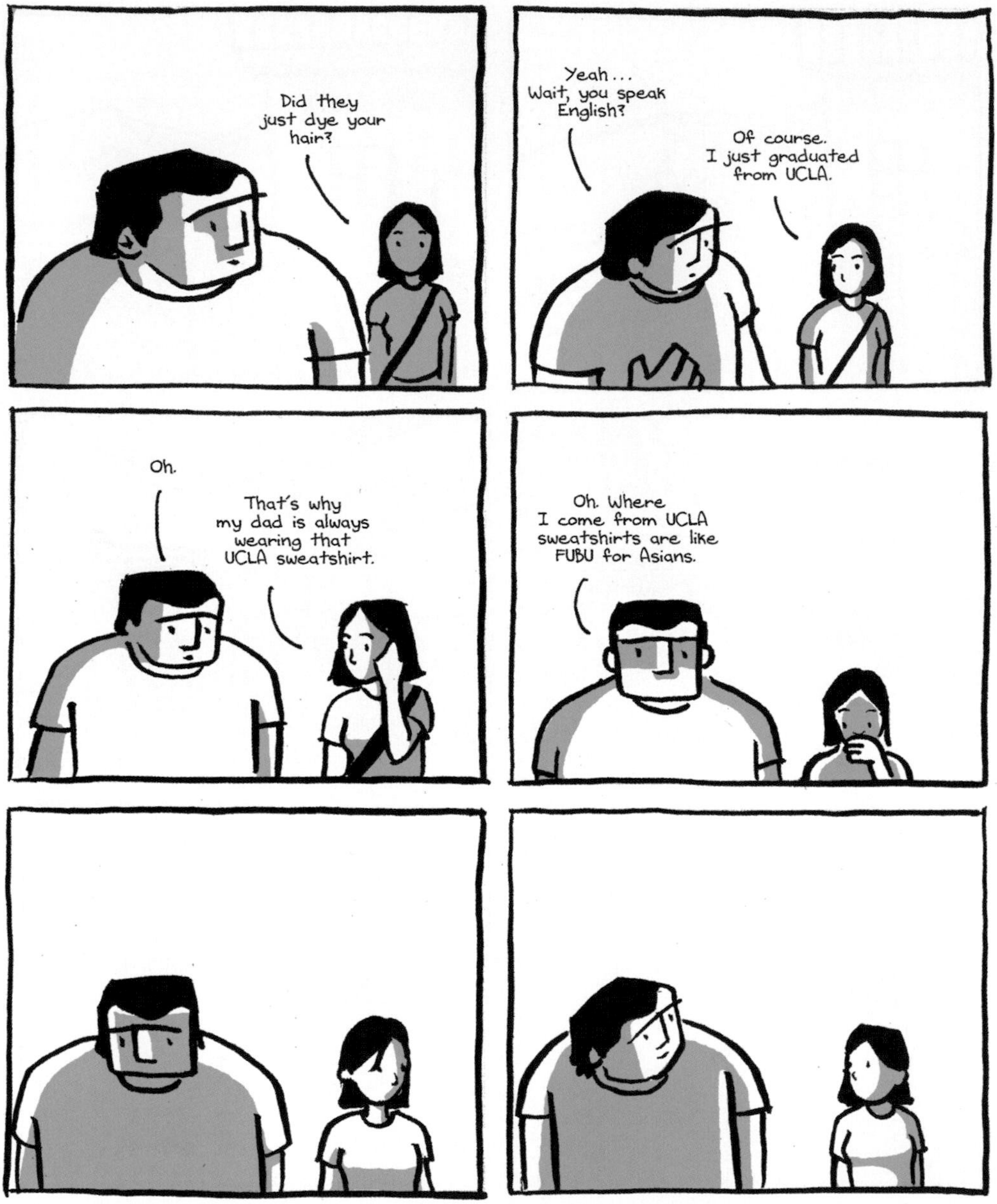
Did they just dye your hair?
Yeah... Wait, you speak English?
Of course. I just graduated from UCLA.
Oh.
That's why my dad is always wearing that UCLA sweatshirt.
Oh. Where I come from UCLA sweatshirts are like FUBU for Asians.

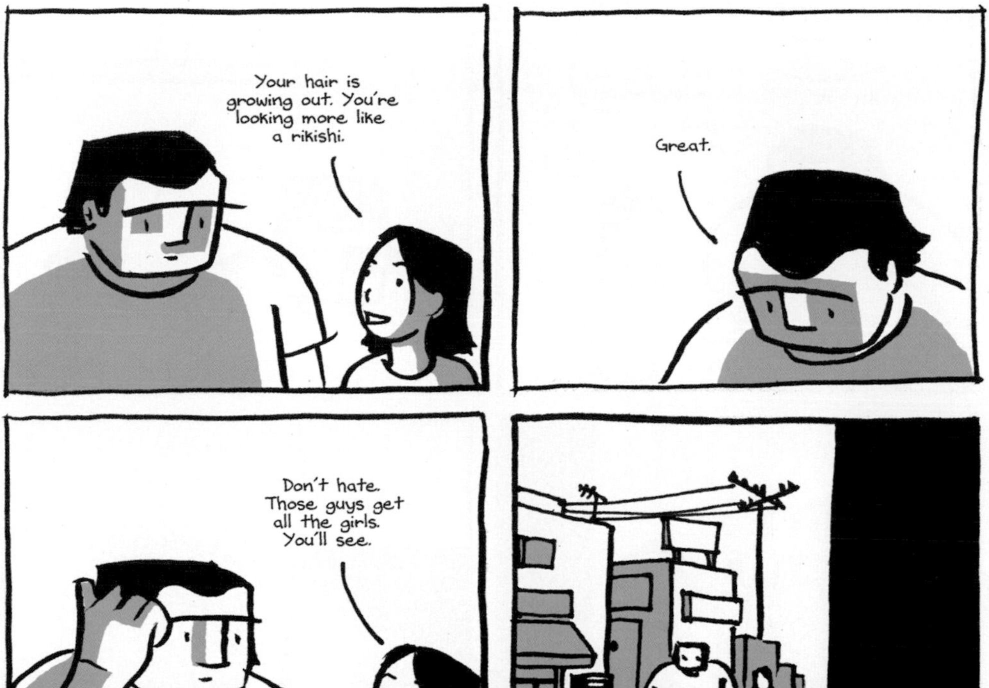
Your hair is growing out. You're looking more like a rikishi.
Great.
Don't hate. Those guys get all the girls. You'll see.
My dad has been talking about you since he went to see you play football.
Really?

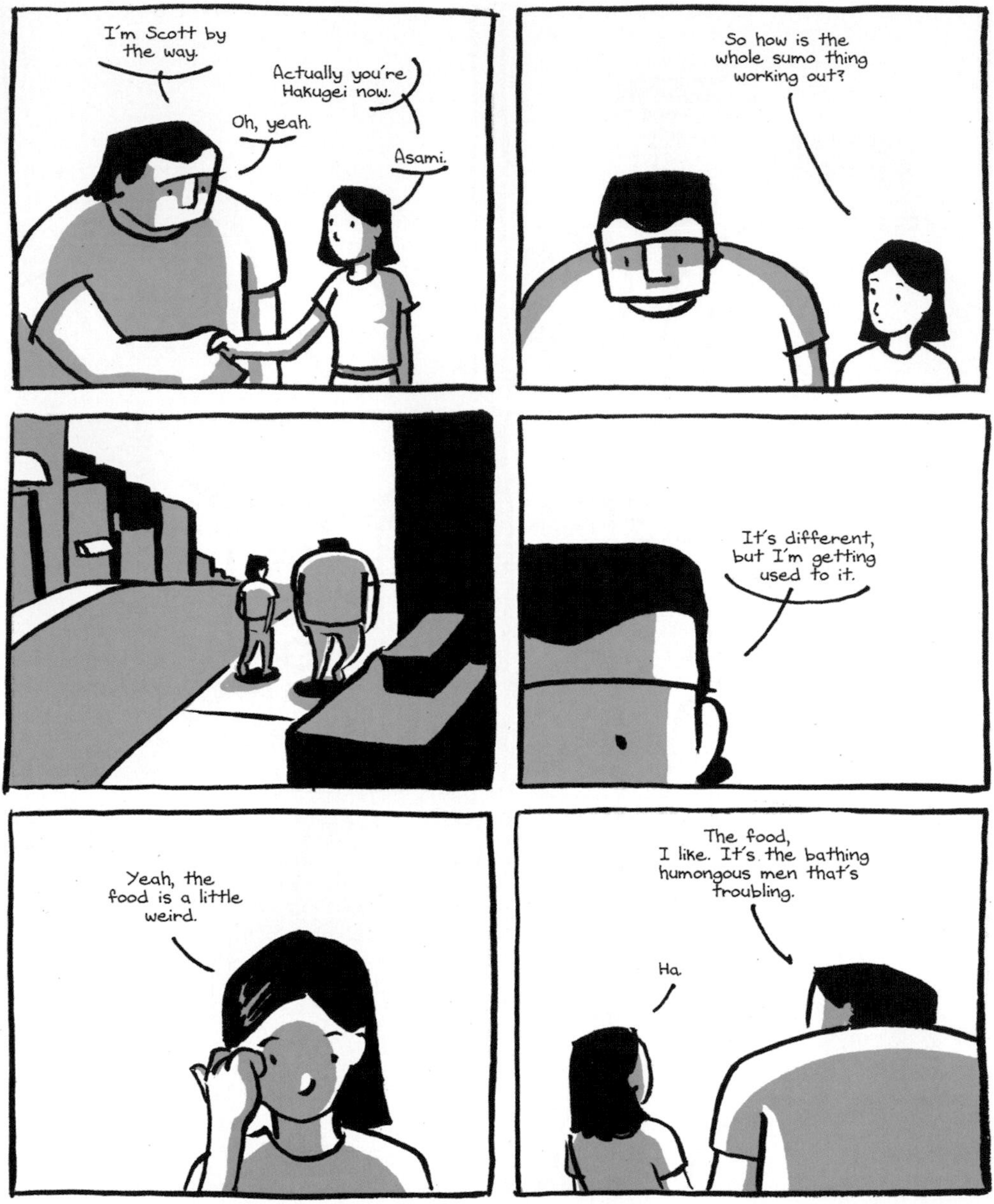
I'm Scott by the way.
Oh, yeah.
Actually you're Hakugei now.
Asami.
So how is the whole sumo thing working out?
It's different, but I'm getting used to it.
Yeah, the food is a little weird.
The food, I like. It's the bathing humongous men that's troubling.
Ha.

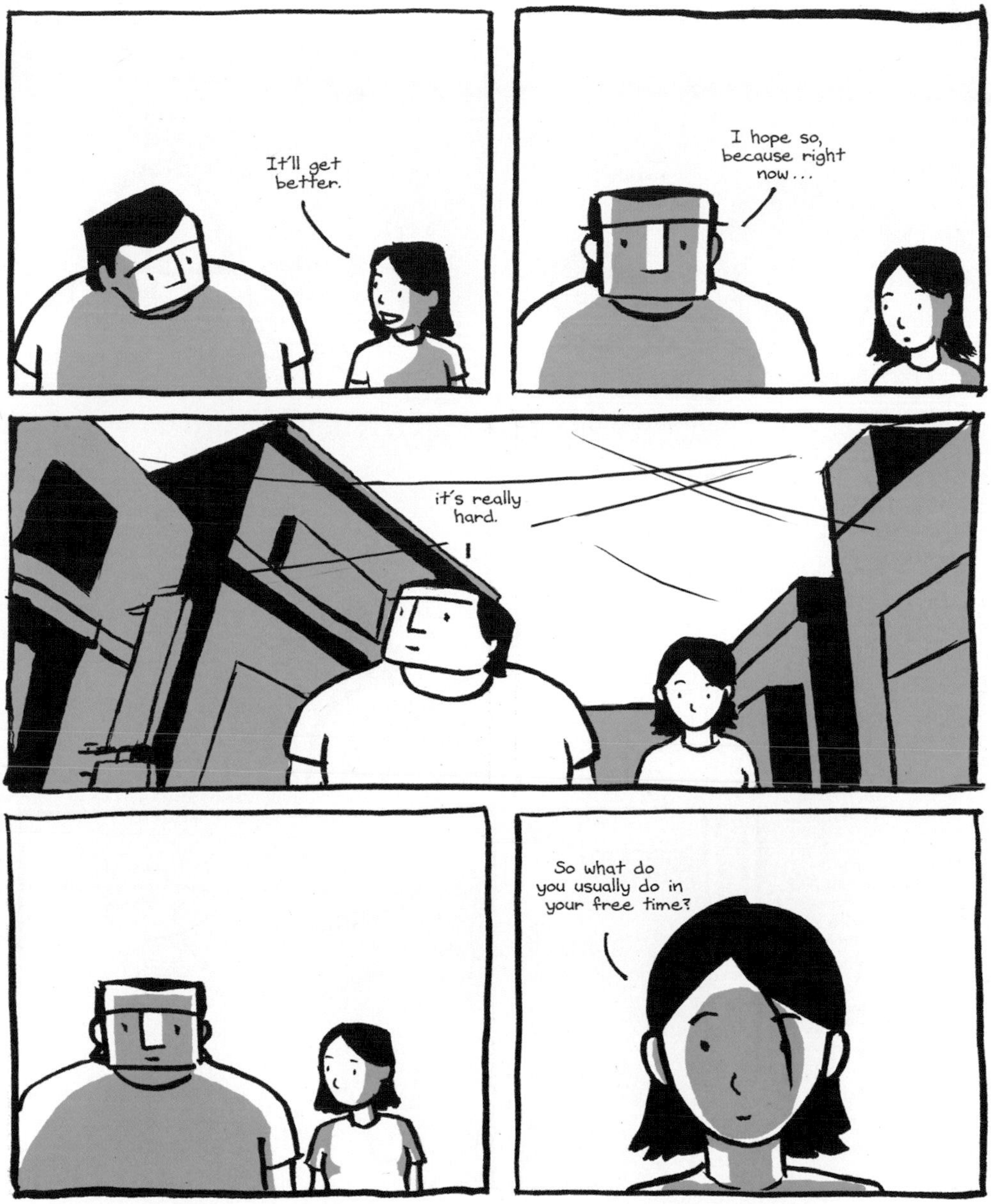
It'll get better.
I hope so, because right now...
it's really hard.
So what do you usually do in your free time?

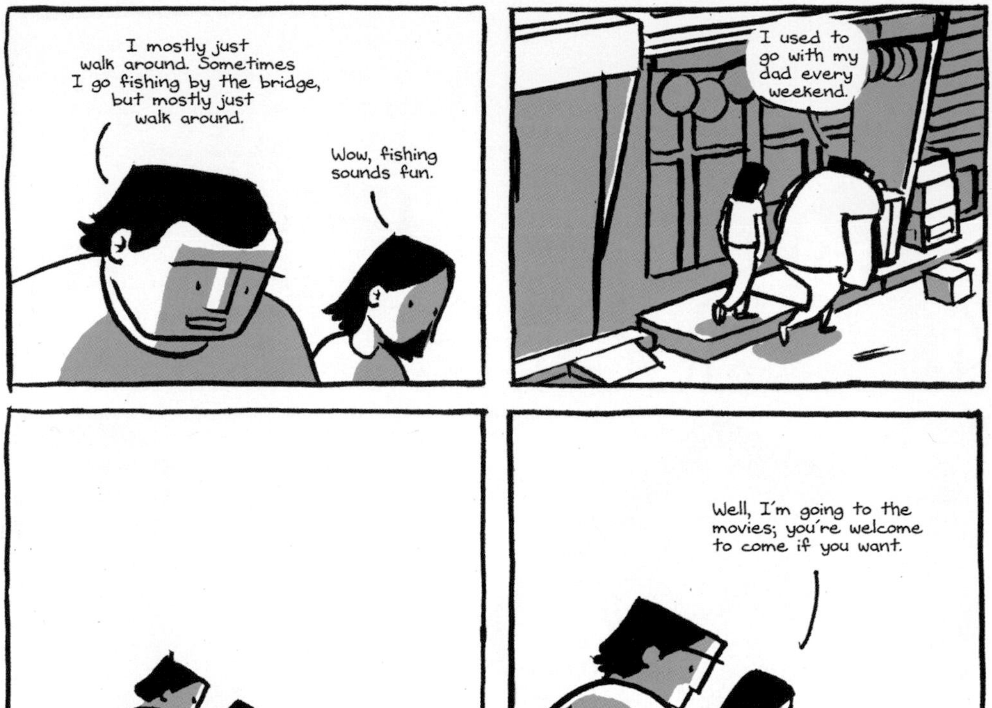
I mostly just walk around. Sometimes I go fishing by the bridge, but mostly just walk around.
Wow, fishing sounds fun.
I used to go with my dad every weekend.
Well, I´m going to the movies; you´re welcome to come if you want.
Yeah? That sounds fun, I haven´t been to the movies in a long time.
I probably won´t understand it, though.

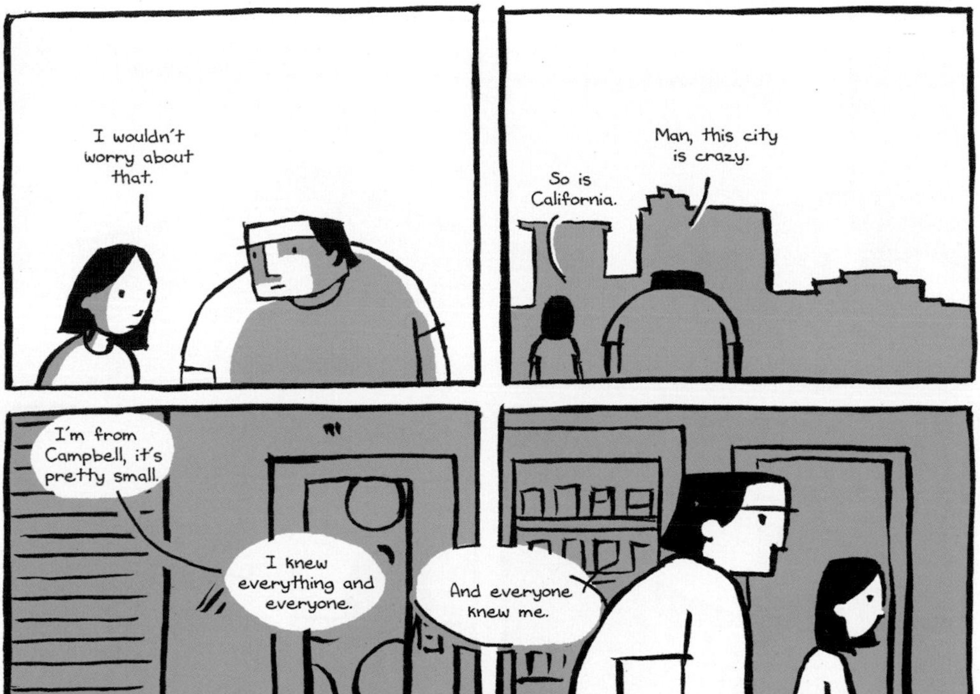
I wouldn't worry about that.
Man, this city is crazy.
So is California.
I'm from Campbell, it's pretty small.
I knew everything and everyone.
And everyone knew me.
But here, I don't know anyone.
Well, now you know me.

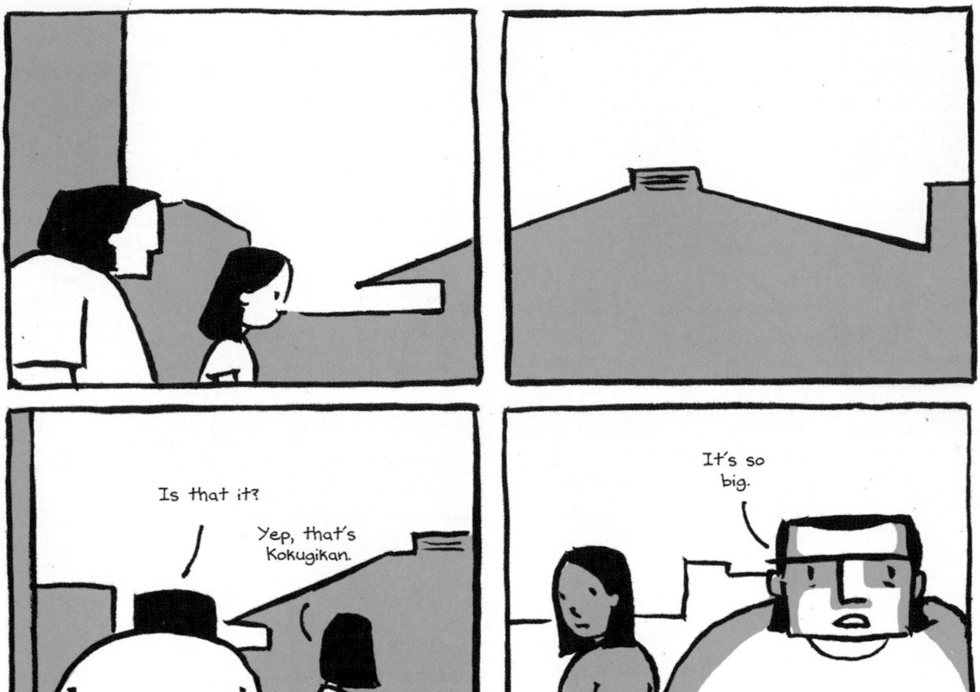
Is that it?
Yep, that's Kokugikan.
It's so big.
You could fit thousands of people in there.
Yeah, sumo isn't doing that well lately though.
Kids these days have no love for tradition. It's all baseball and UFC now.

Even our theaters play American movies.
ART
KARATE KID II
I knew that would cheer you up.
Oh hey! I just realized I have no money.
Hows about I make you a deal. I'll pay for the movie if you take me fishing sometime.
Two, please.

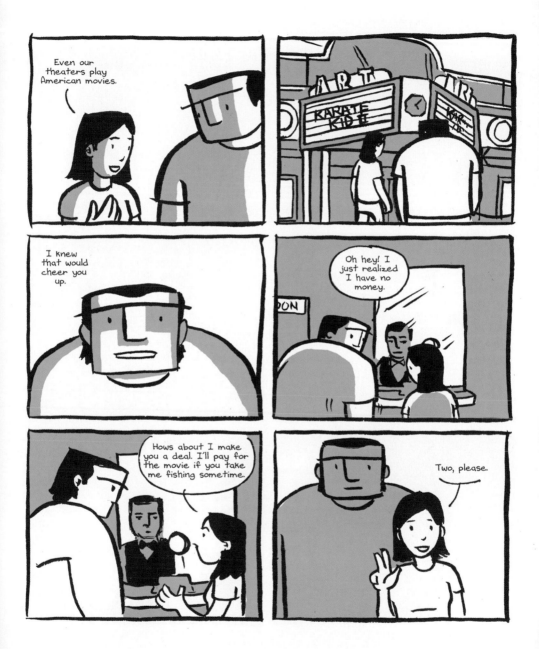

Tsa!

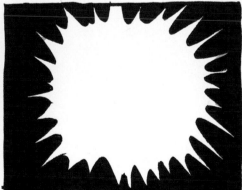

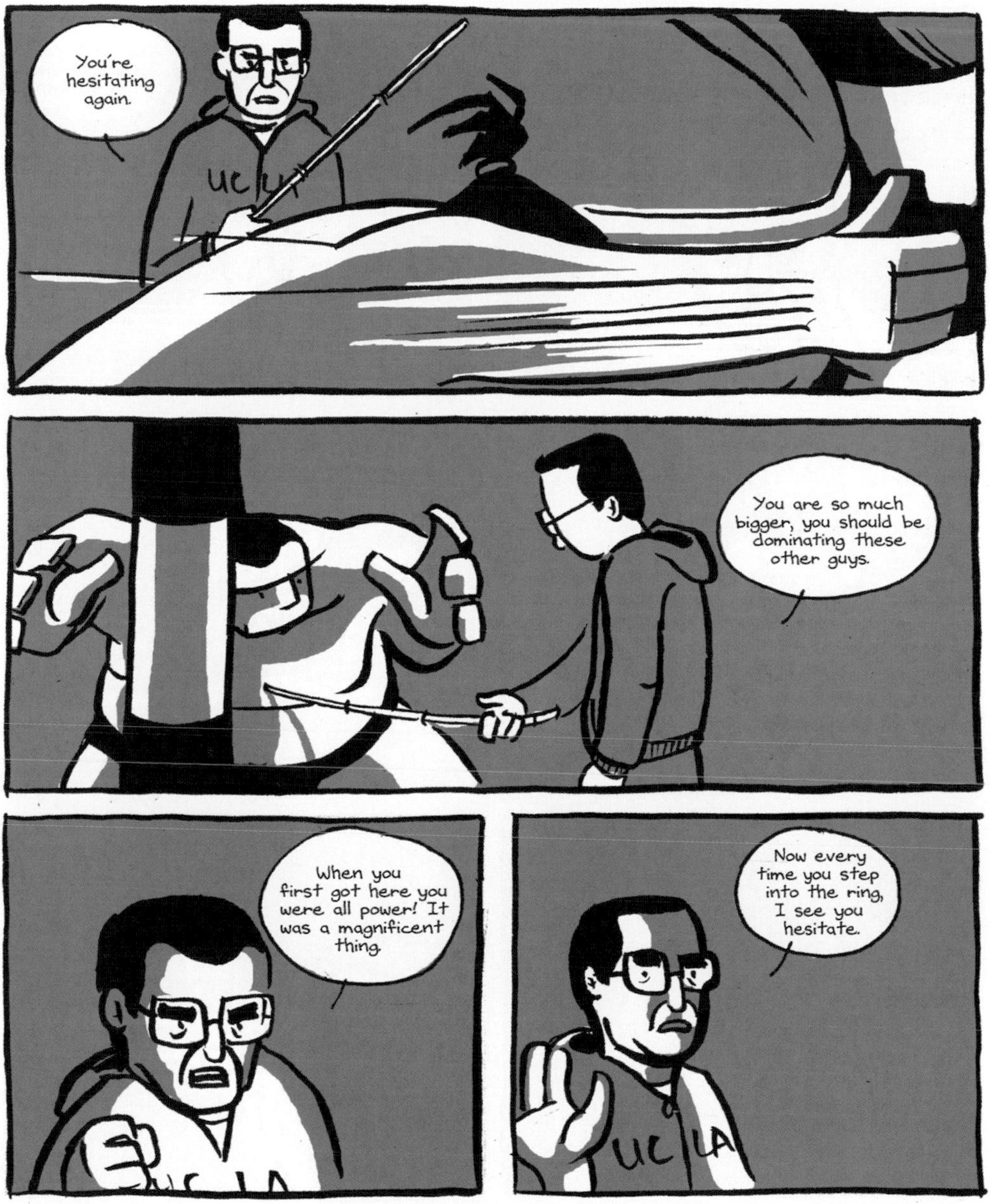
You're hesitating again.
UC LA
You are so much bigger, you should be dominating these other guys.
When you first got here you were all power! It was a magnificent thing.
Now every time you step into the ring, I see you hesitate.
UC LA

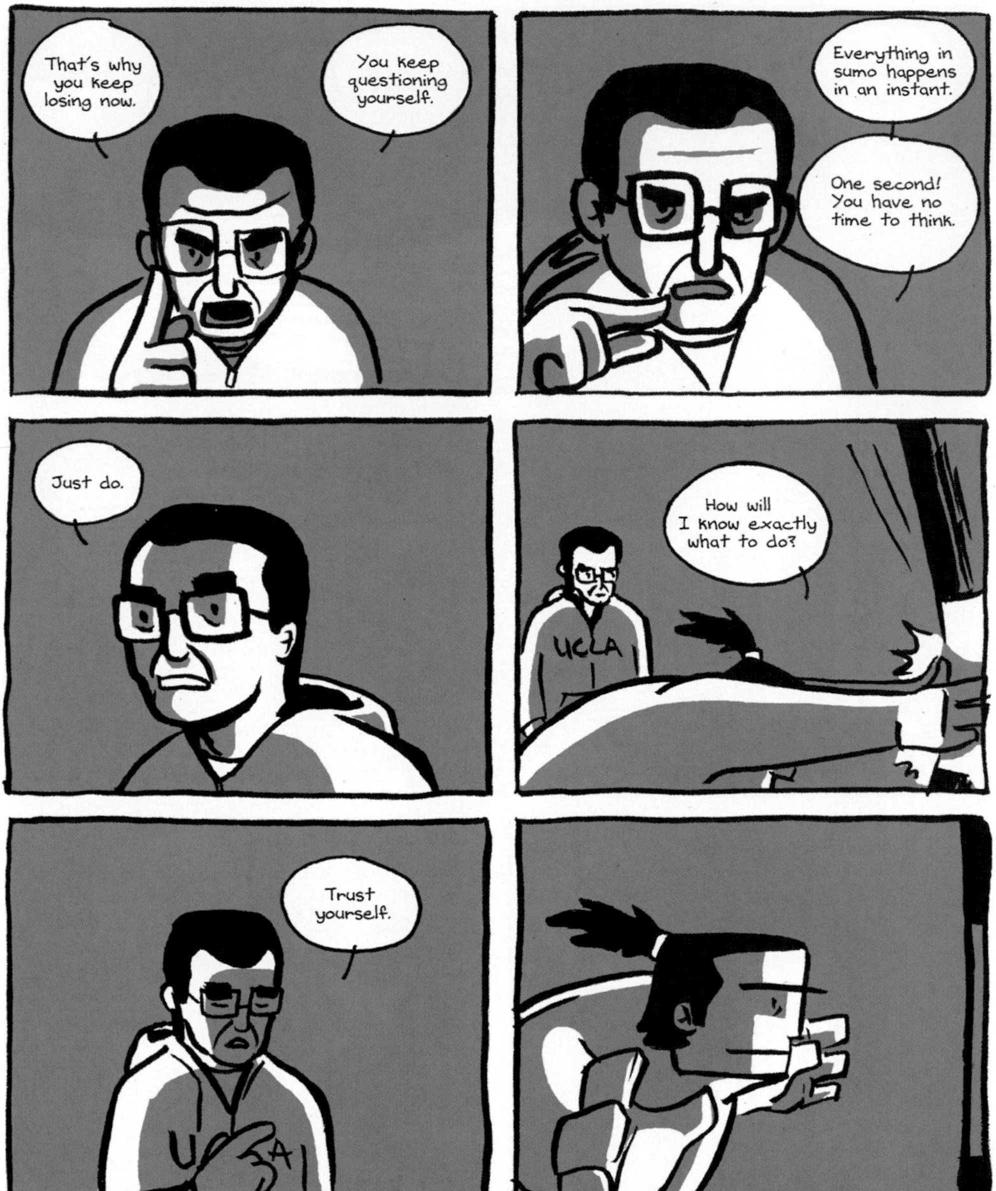
That's why you keep losing now.
You keep questioning yourself.
Everything in sumo happens in an instant.
One second! You have no time to think.
Just do.
How will I know exactly what to do?
UCLA
Trust yourself.

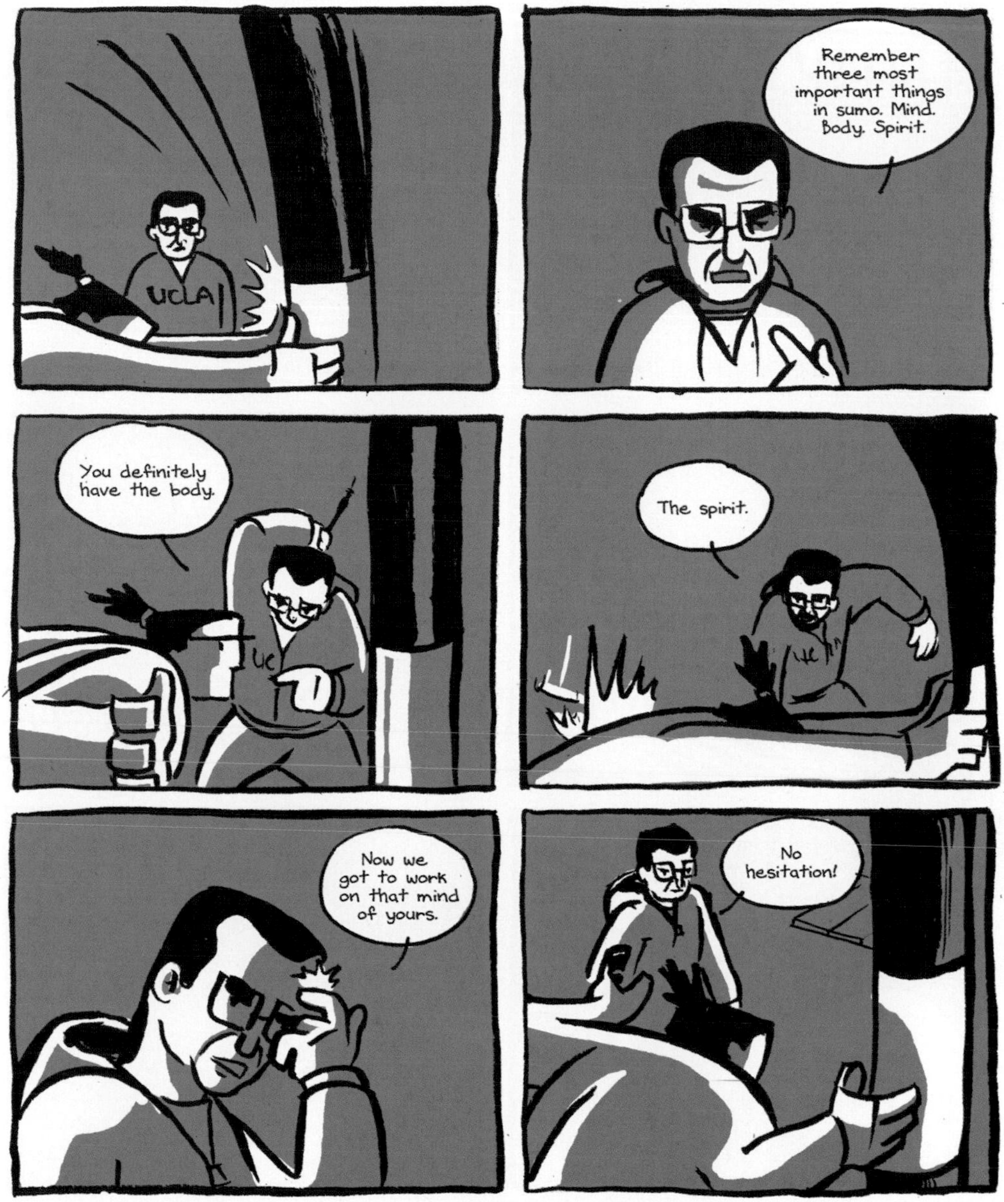
UCLA
Remember three most important things in sumo. Mind. Body. Spirit.
You definitely have the body.
UC
The spirit.
Now we got to work on that mind of yours.
No hesitation!

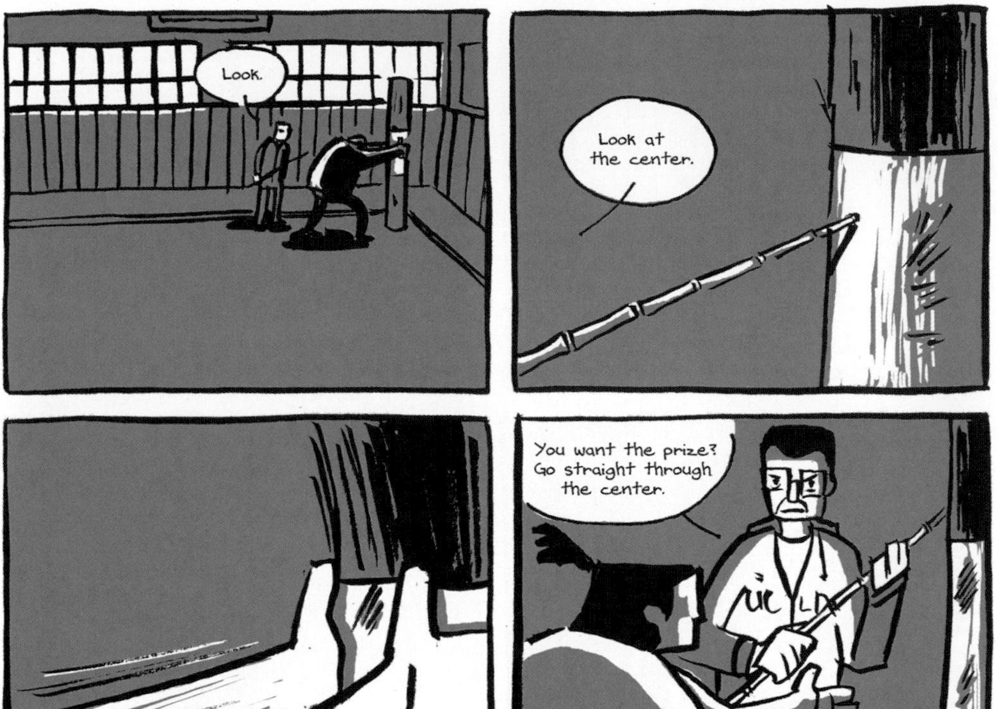
Look.
Look at the center.
You want the prize? Go straight through the center.
No hesitating, no going around. Meet it straight on.

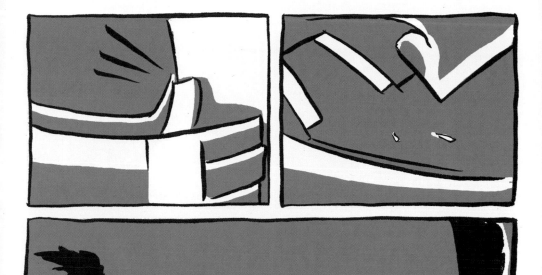

Tomorrow's match is the most important of your career. You've been moving up and down the lower ranks for too long. If you don't move up now, it's going to be too late.

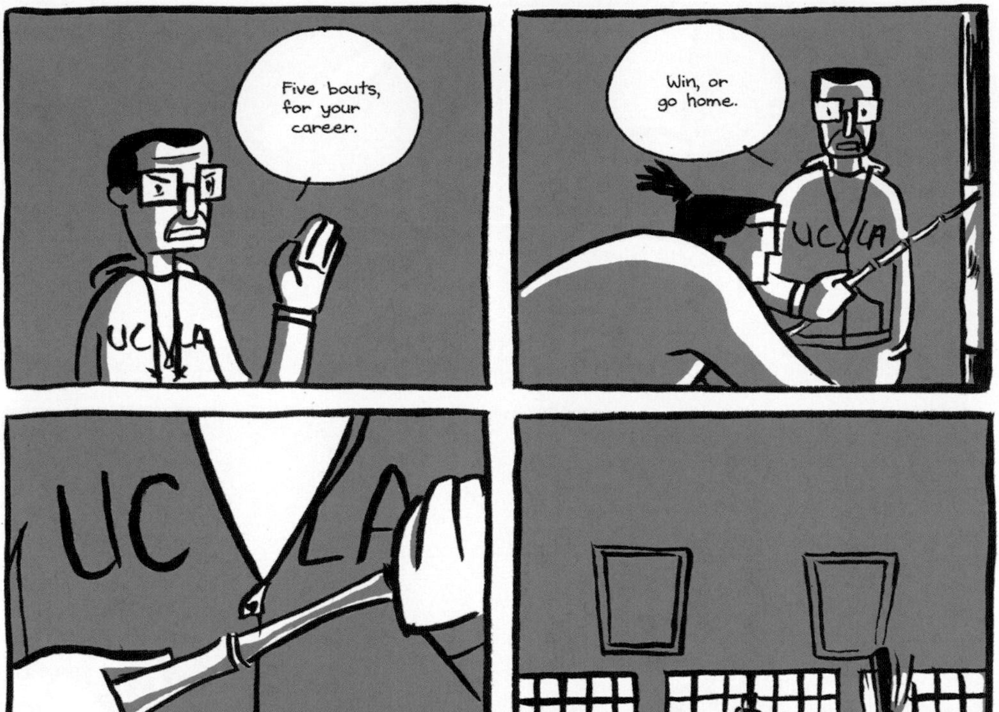
Five bouts, for your career.
UCLA
Win, or go home.
UCLA
UCLA
This is the moment of truth.
Every moment is the moment of truth.

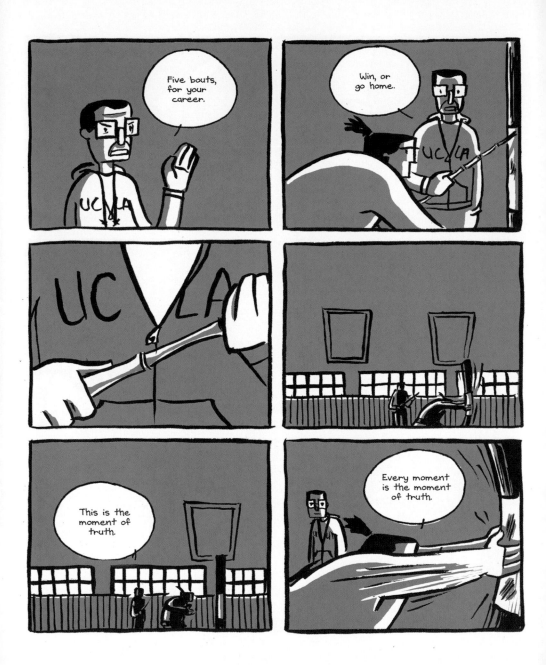

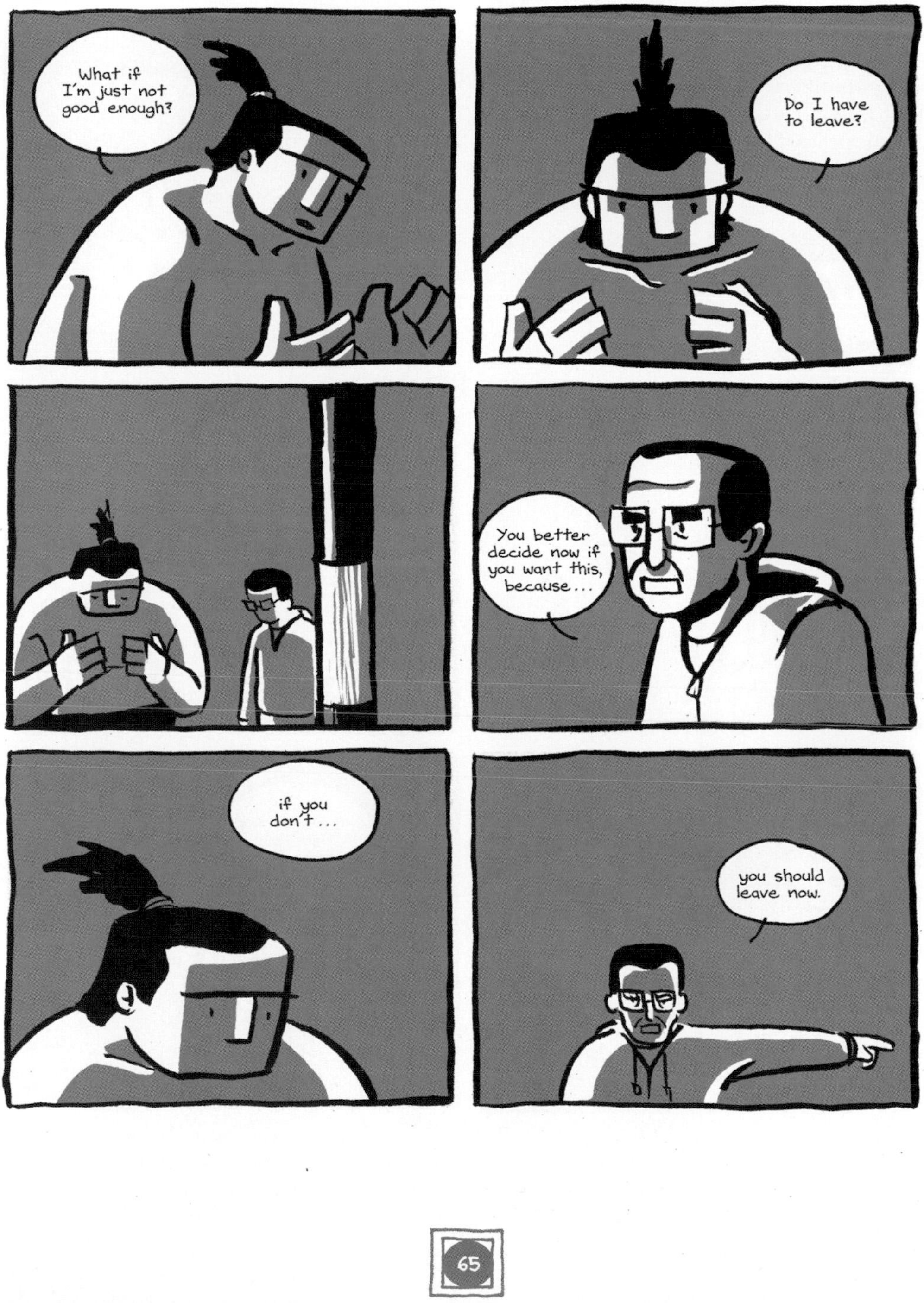
What if I'm just not good enough?
Do I have to leave?
You better decide now if you want this, because...
if you don't...
you should leave now.

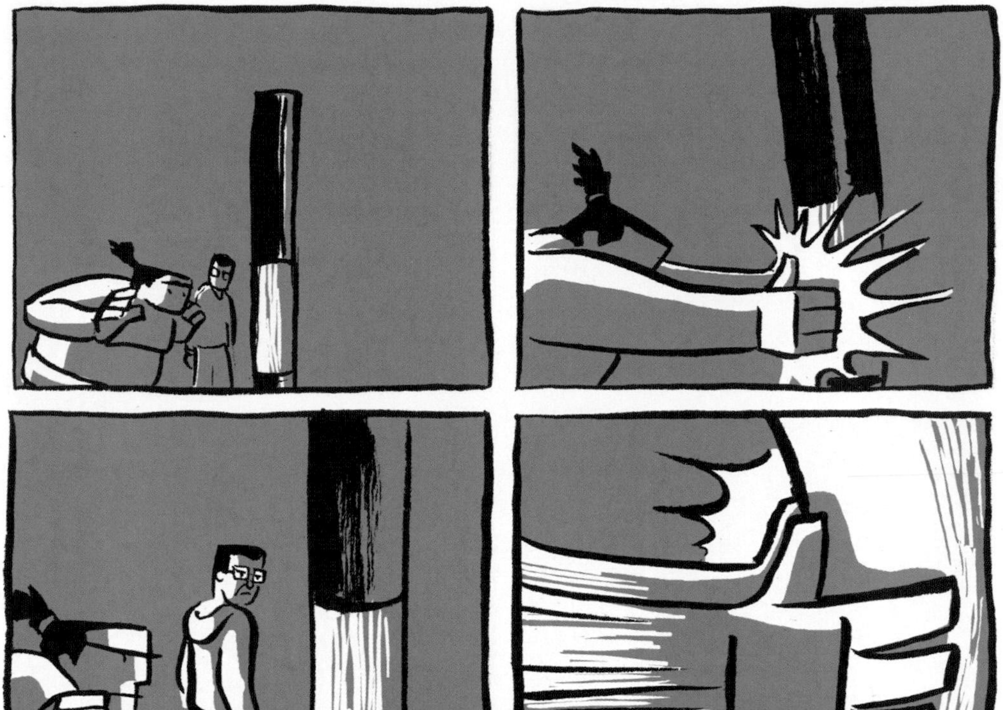
I want this.
Then get me that win.
UCLA

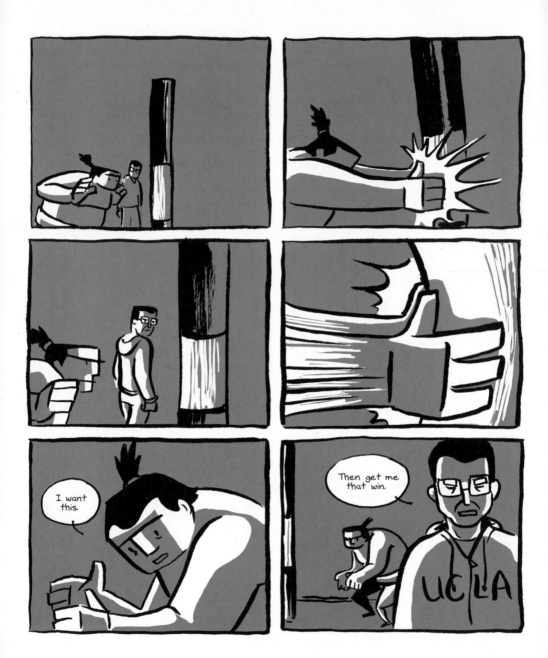

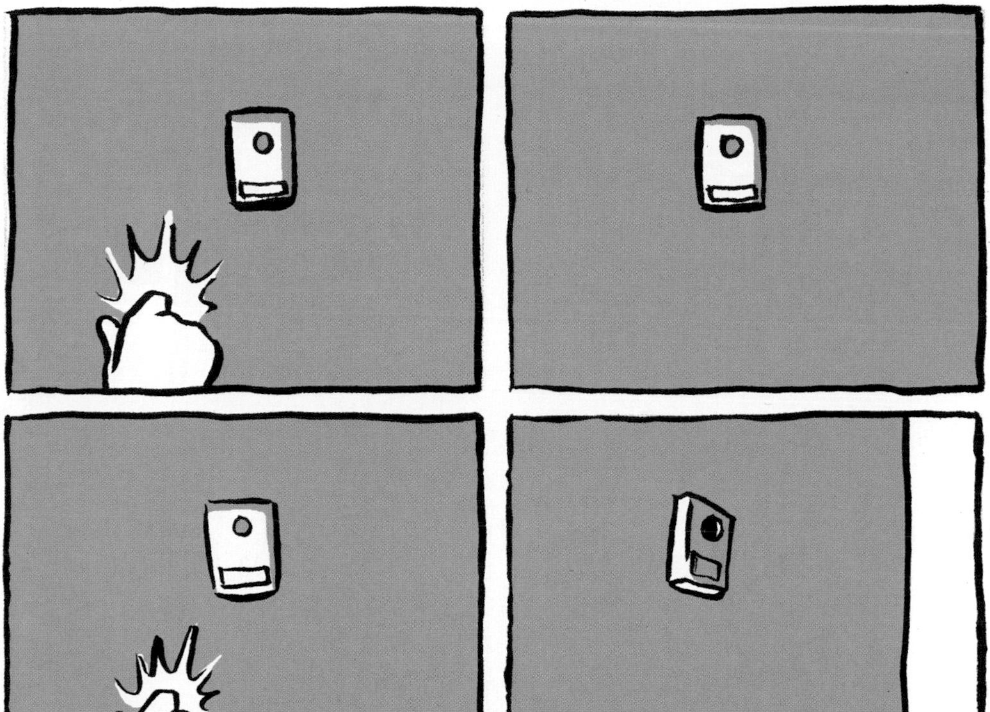
Gwen.
Hey, you didn't call last night.

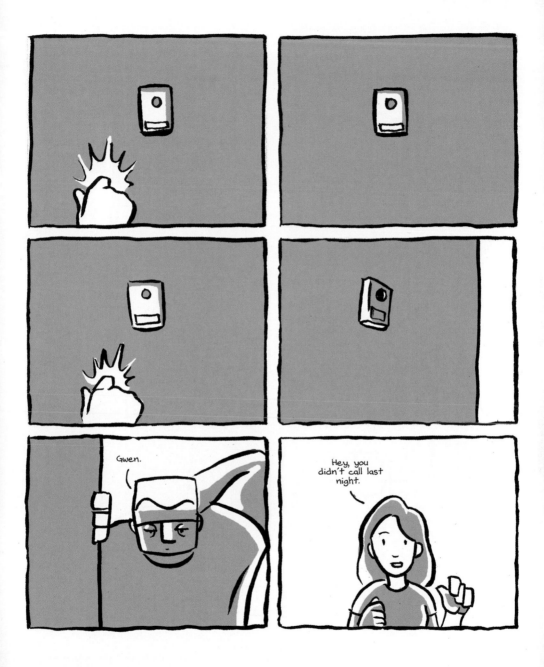

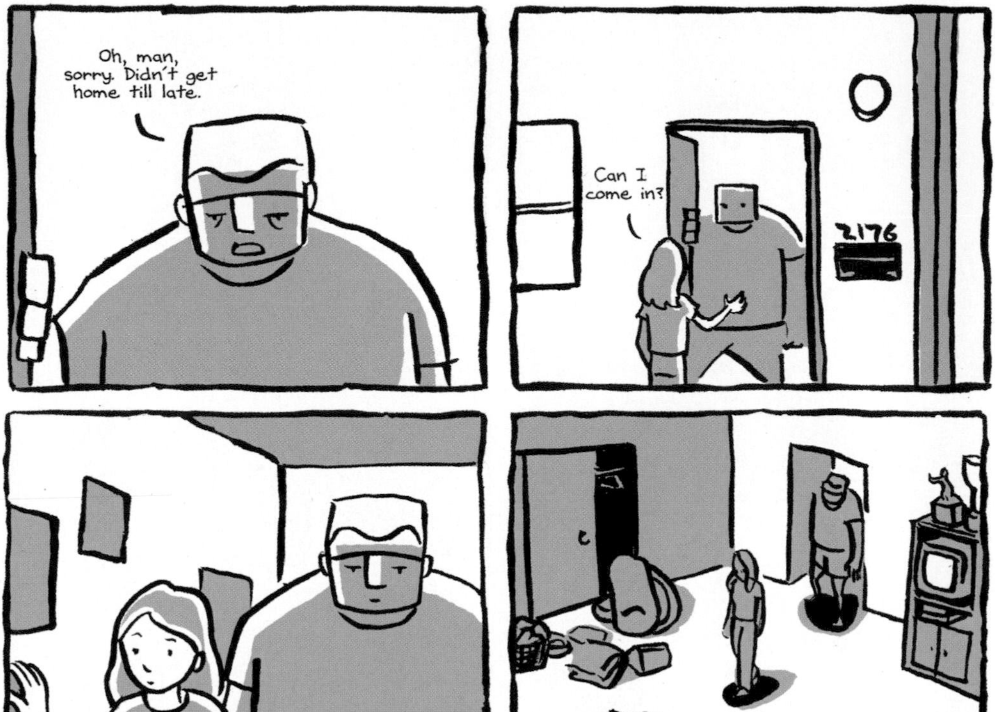
Oh, man, sorry. Didn't get home till late.
Can I come in?
2176
So, what's up?
Well, I've been doing a lot of thinking lately, and . . .

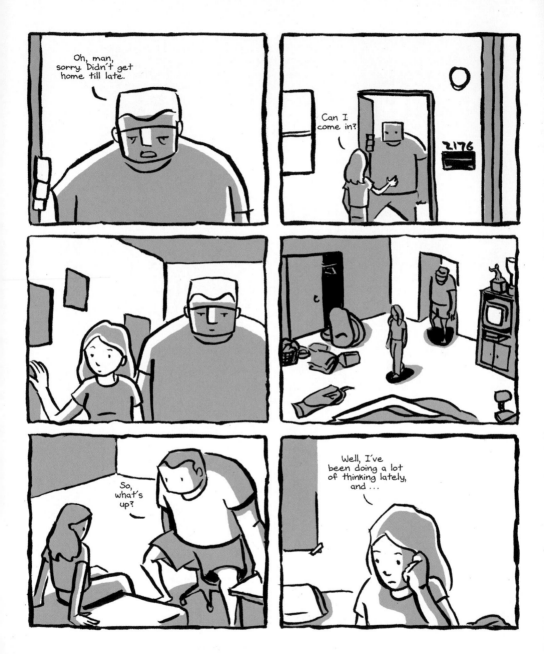

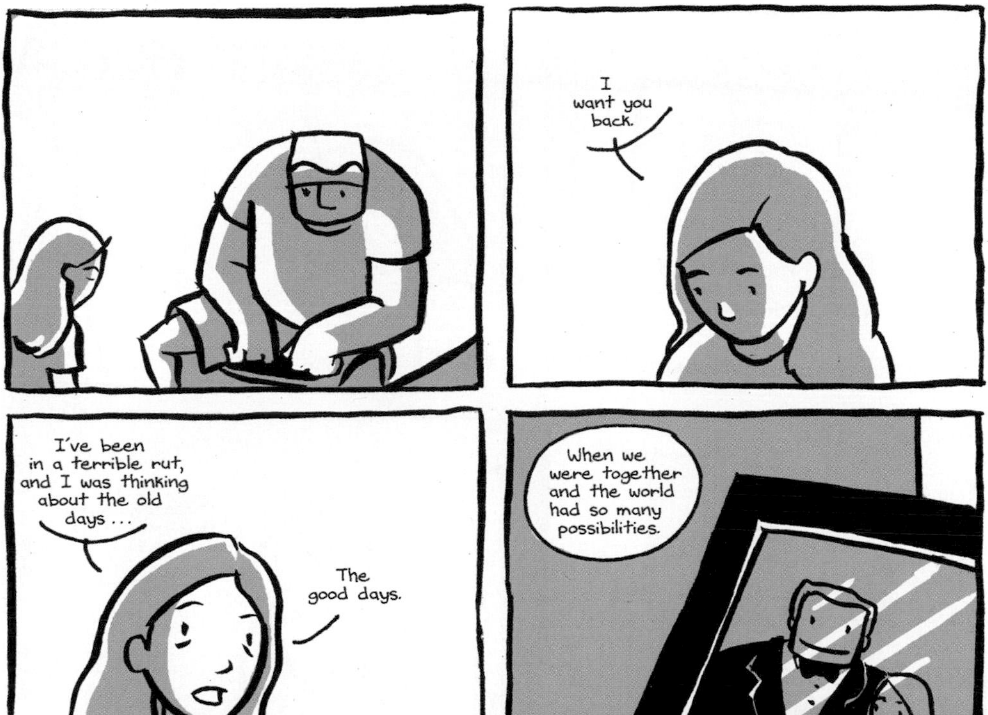
I want you back.
I've been in a terrible rut, and I was thinking about the old days . . .
The good days.
When we were together and the world had so many possibilities.
The football star and the homecoming queen . . . all that.
Those were great days.
C.C.S PLAYER of THE YEAR
And . . .

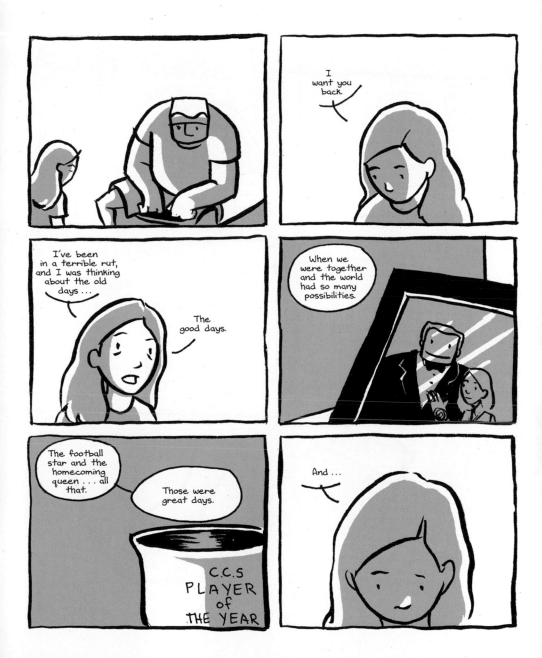

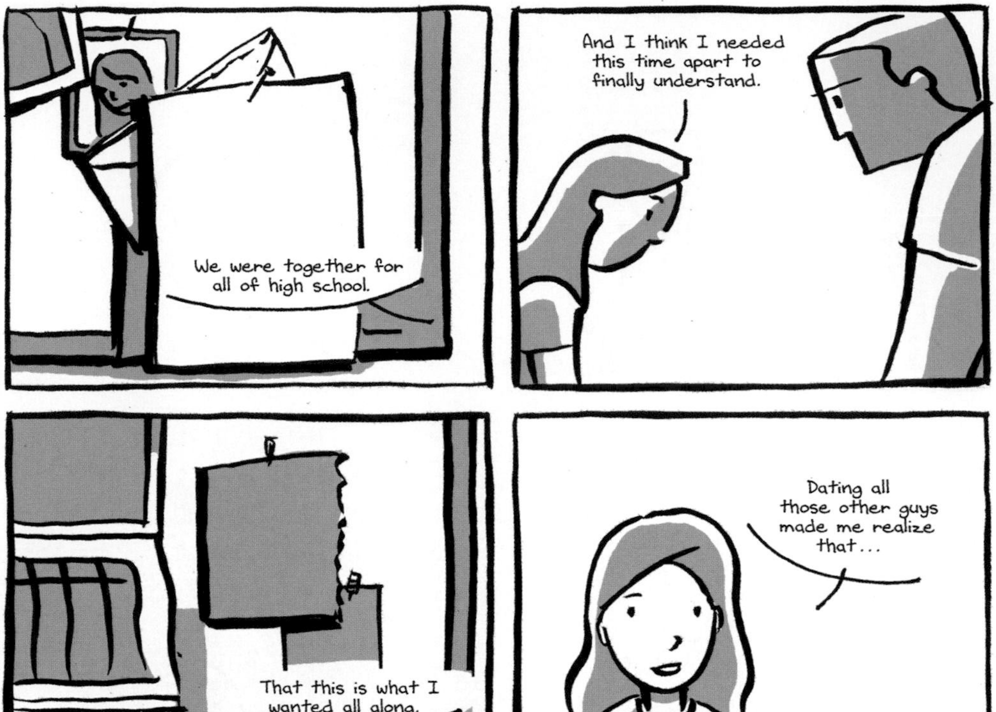
We were together for all of high school.
And I think I needed this time apart to finally understand.
That this is what I wanted all along.
Dating all those other guys made me realize that...
All those other guys?
You're the one.

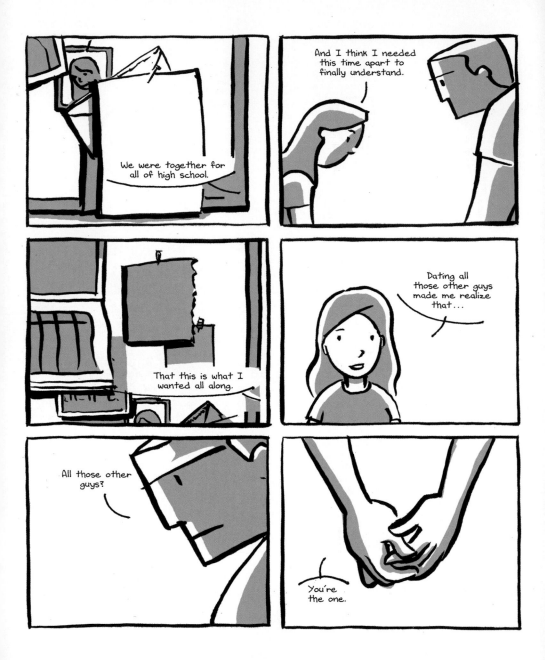

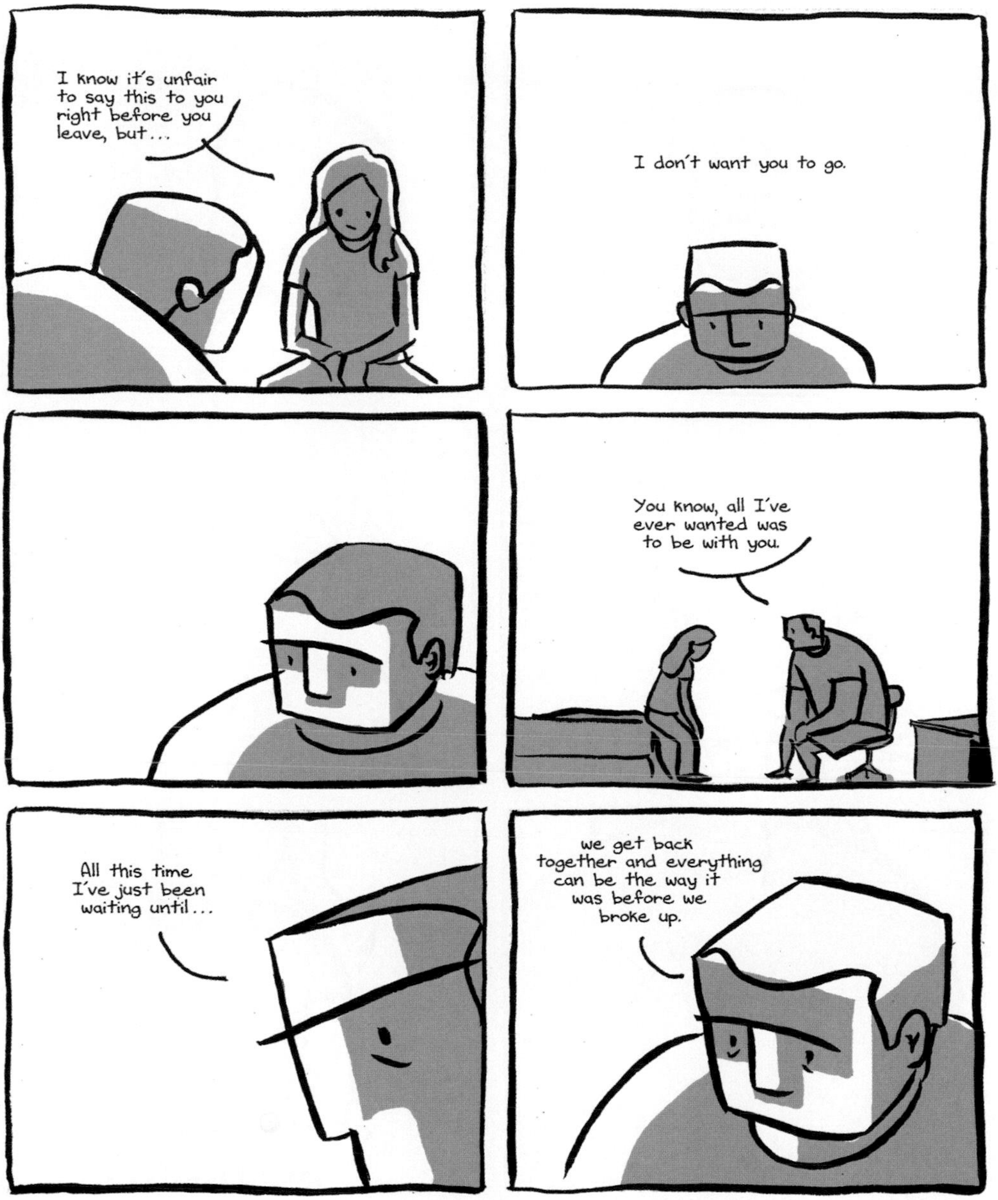
I know it's unfair to say this to you right before you leave, but...
I don't want you to go.
You know, all I've ever wanted was to be with you.
All this time I've just been waiting until...
we get back together and everything can be the way it was before we broke up.

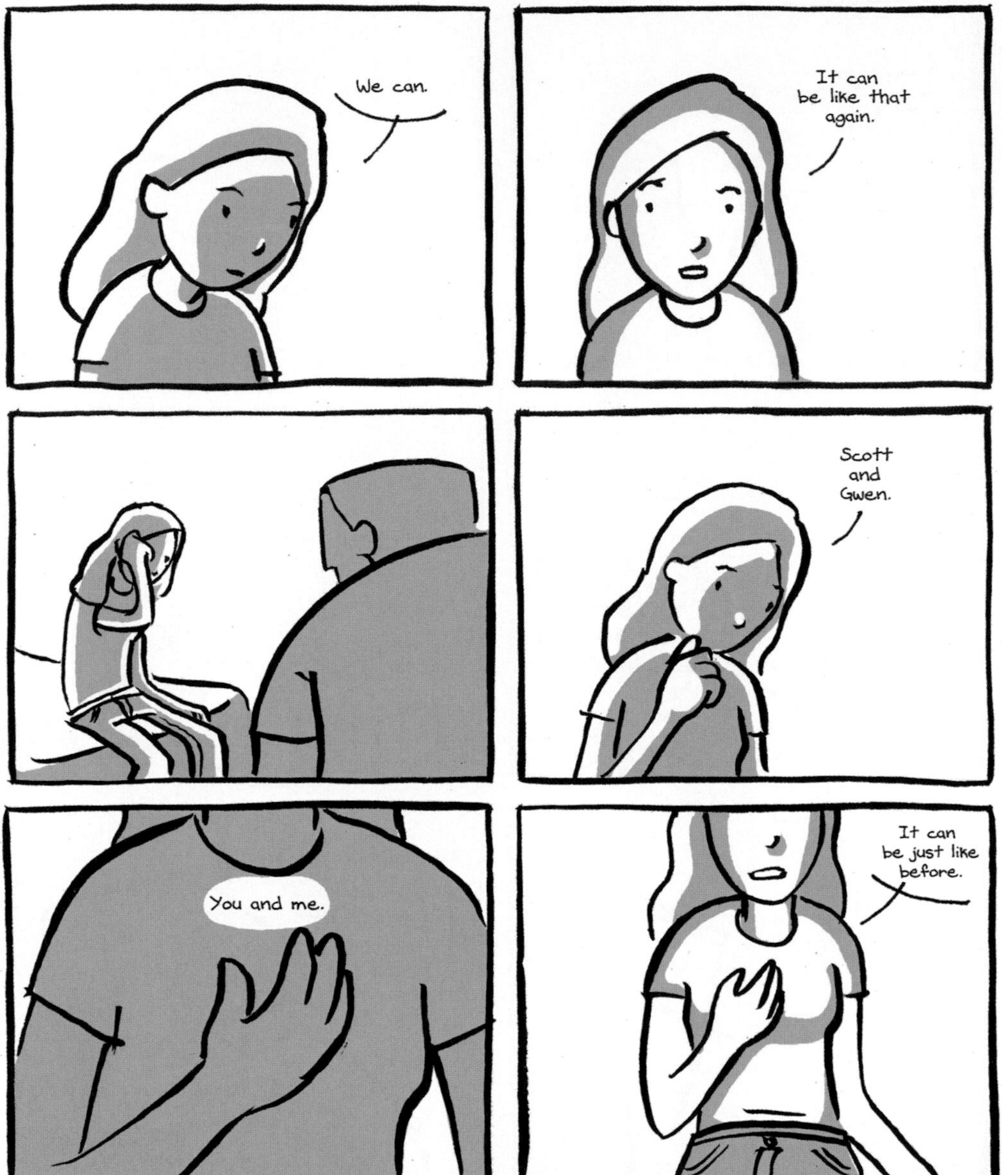
We can.
It can be like that again.
Scott and Gwen.
You and me.
It can be just like before.

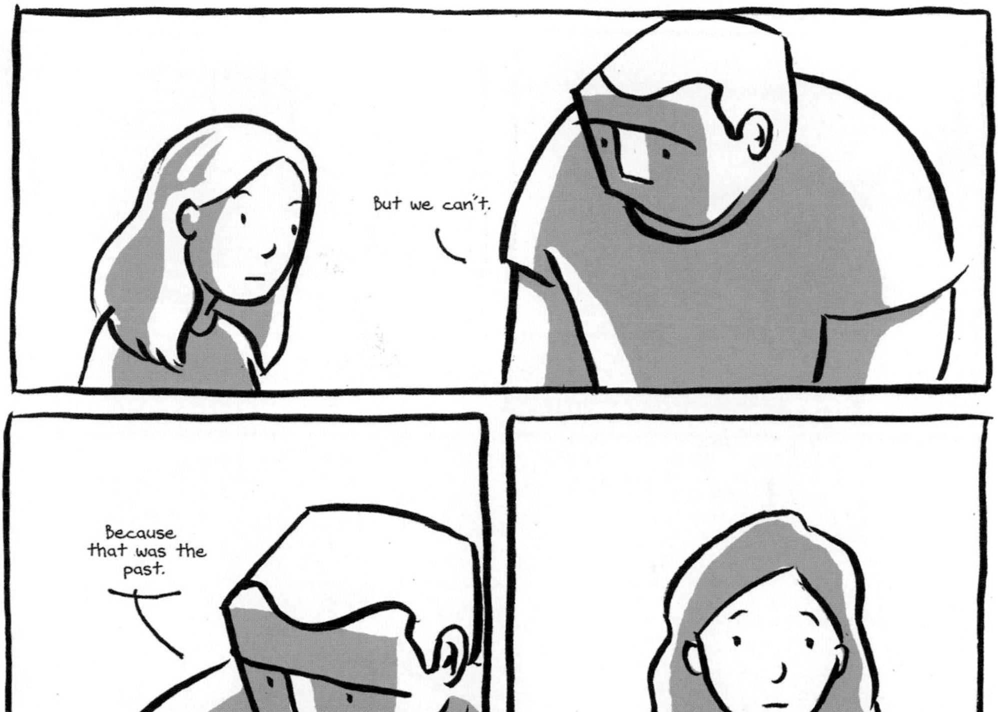
But we can't.
Because that was the past.
We can't just relive the past...

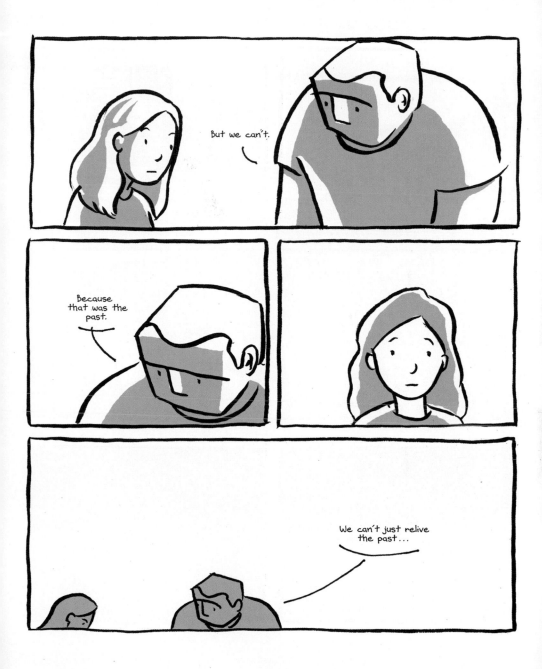

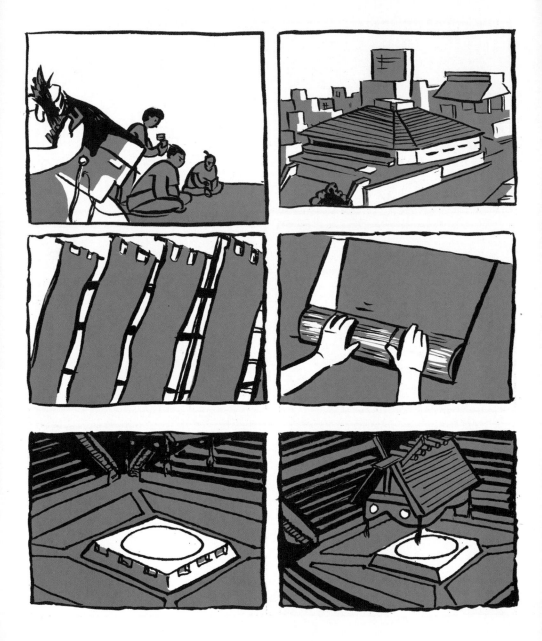

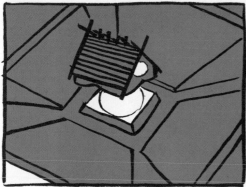

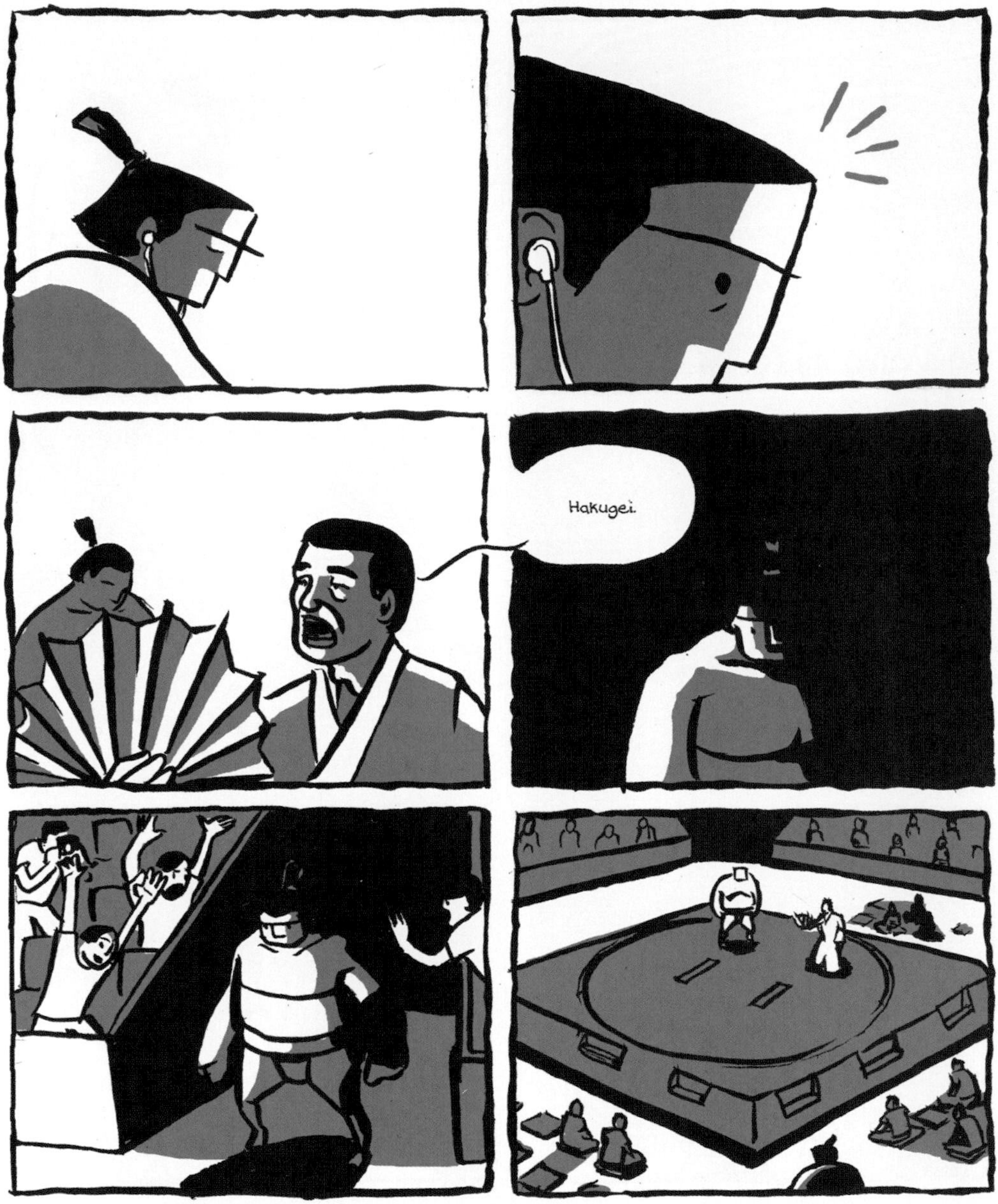
Hakugei.

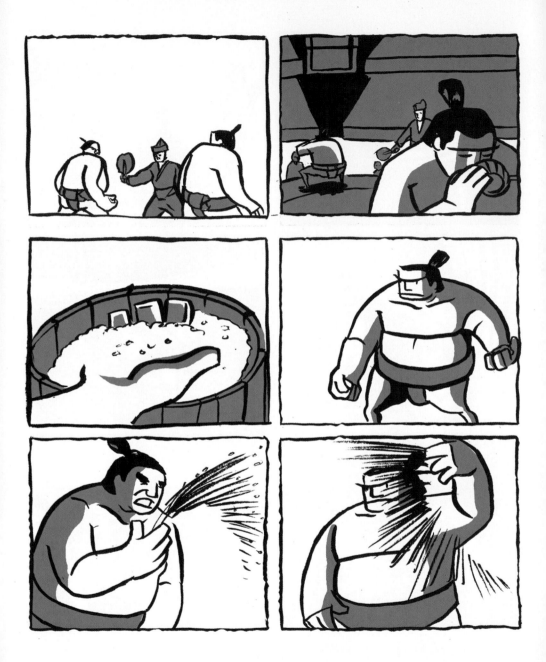

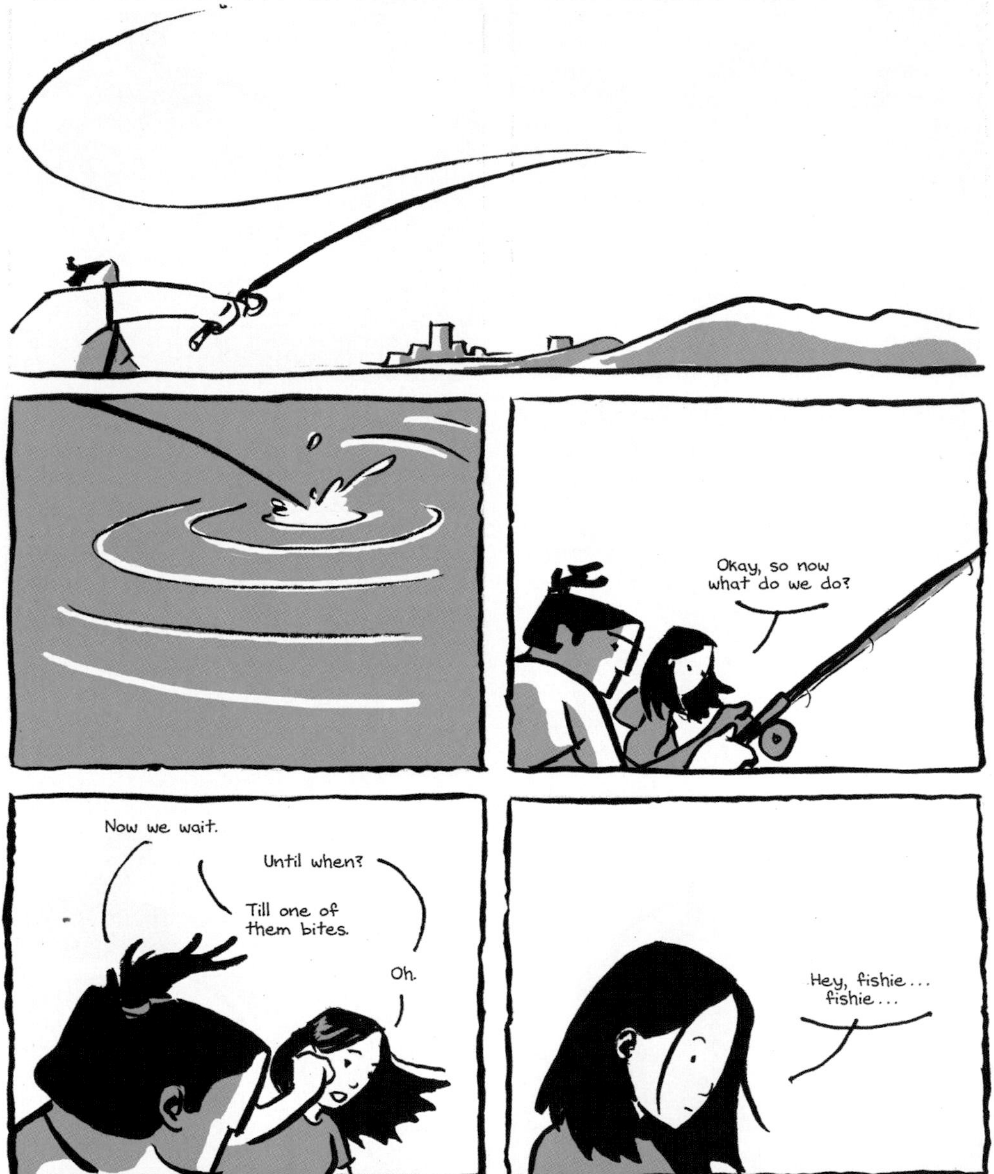
Okay, so now what do we do?
Now we wait.
Until when?
Till one of them bites.
Oh.
Hey, fishie... fishie...

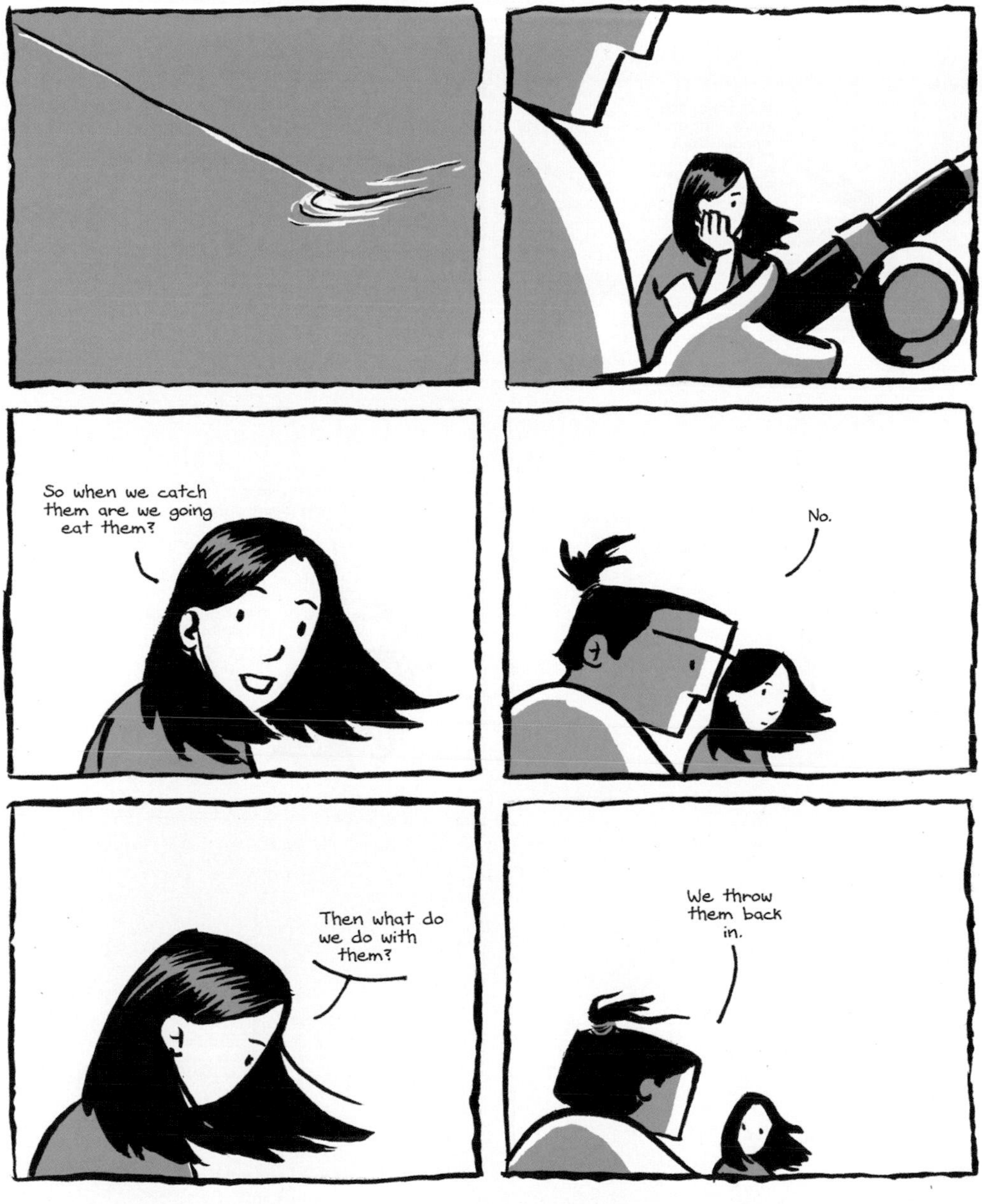
So when we catch them are we going eat them?
No.
Then what do we do with them?
We throw them back in.

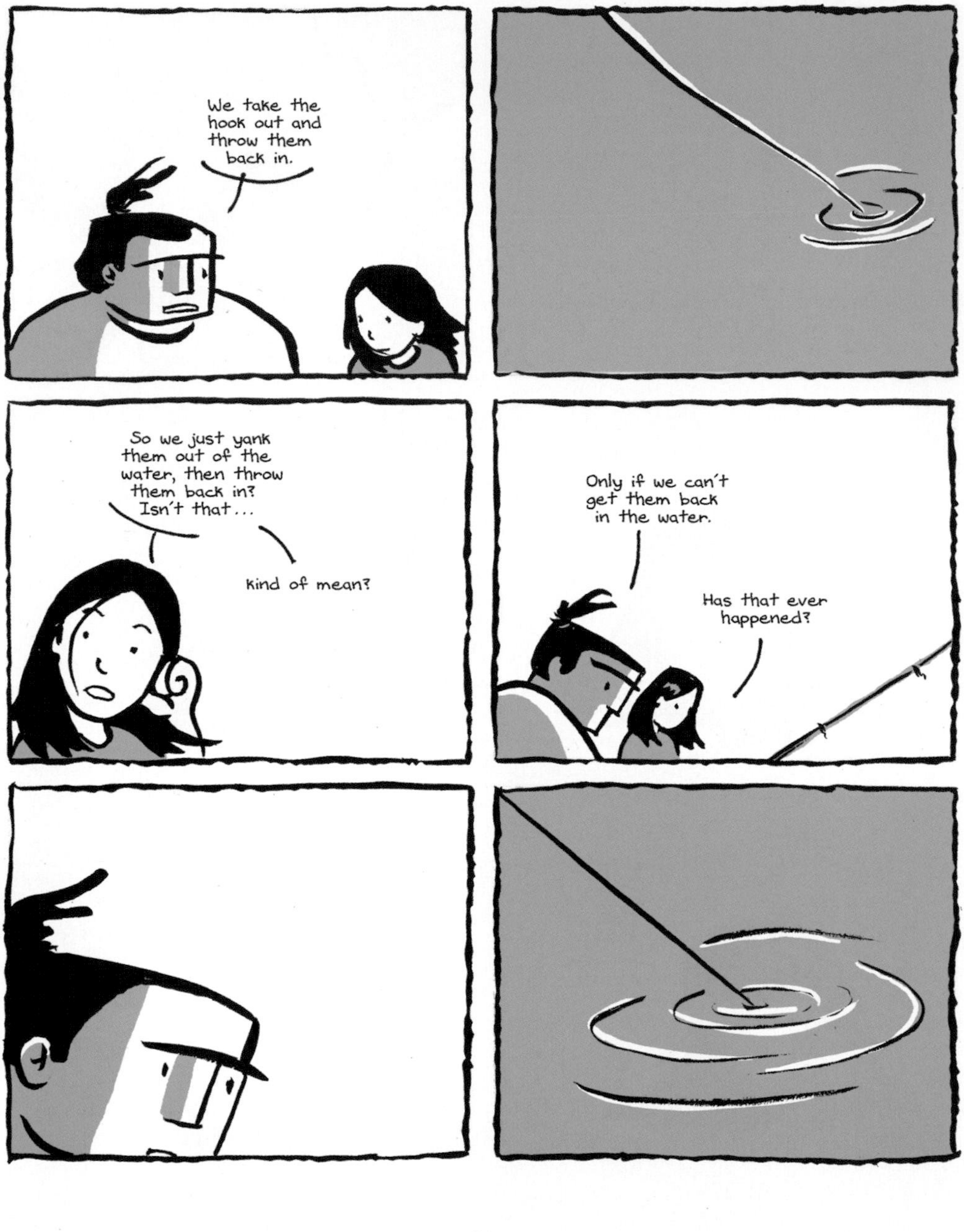
We take the hook out and throw them back in.
So we just yank them out of the water, then throw them back in? Isn't that...
Kind of mean?
Only if we can't get them back in the water.
Has that ever happened?

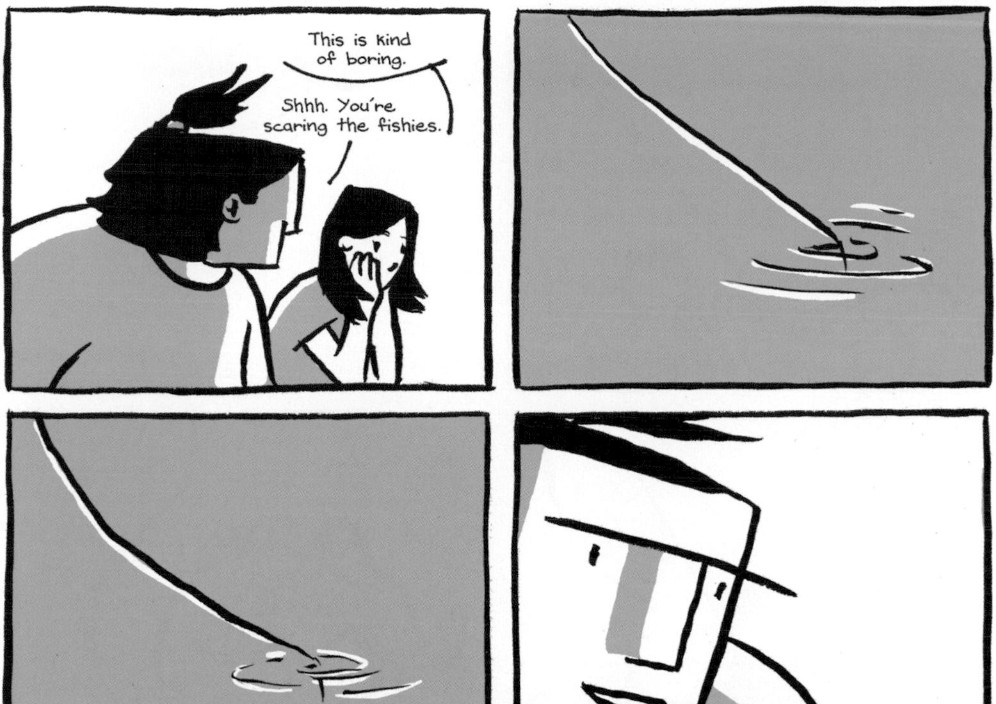
This is kind of boring.
Shhh. You're scaring the fishies.
You have to be patient. They'll come.

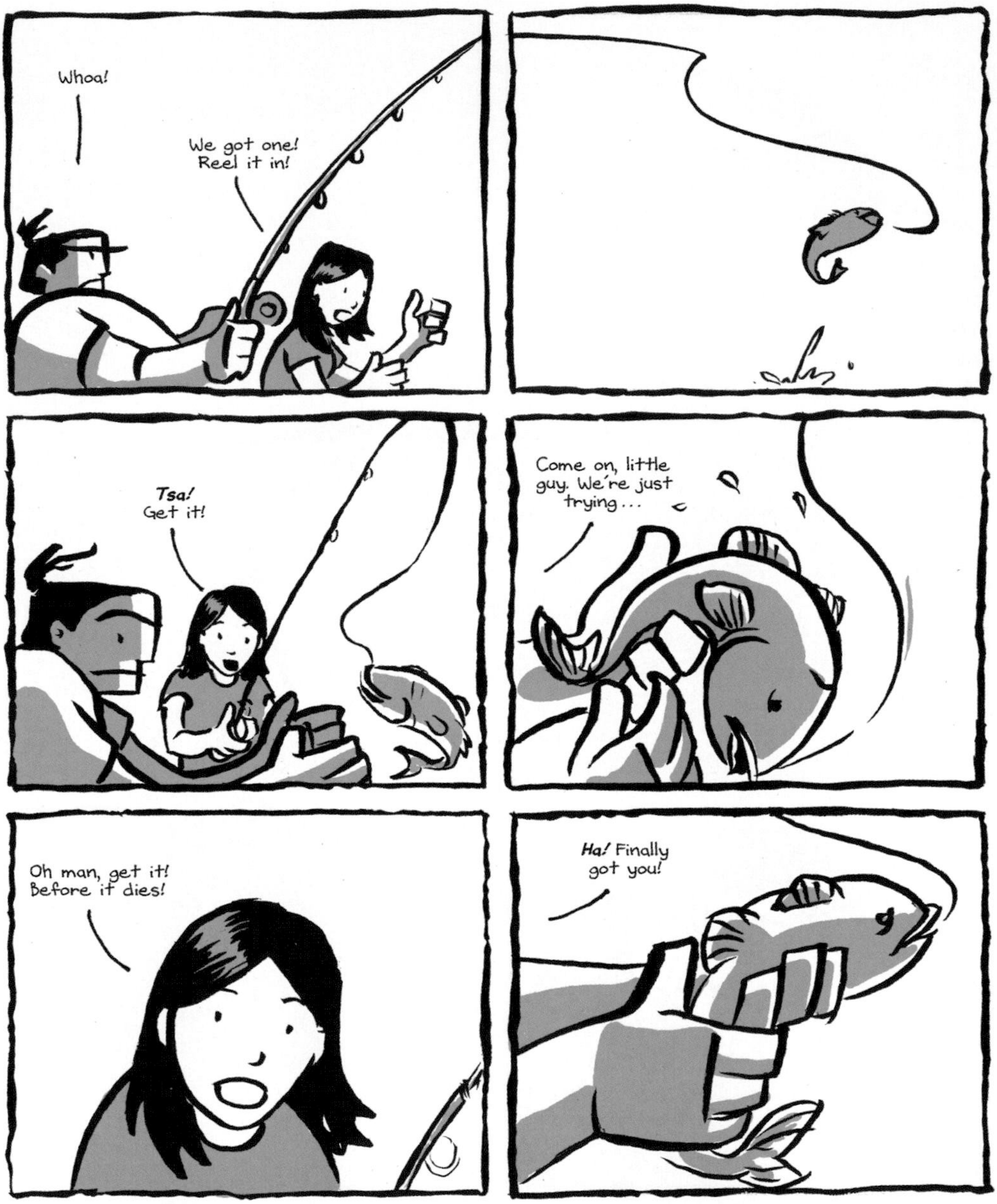
Whoa!
We got one! Reel it in!
Tsa! Get it!
Come on, little guy. We're just trying...
Oh man, get it! Before it dies!
Ha! Finally got you!

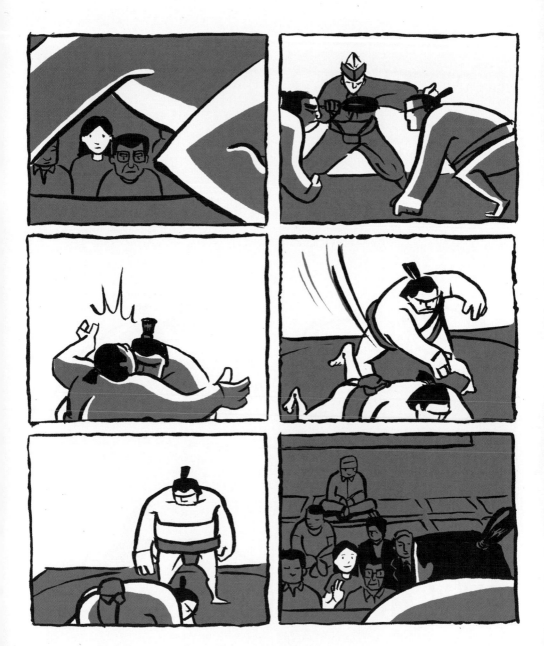

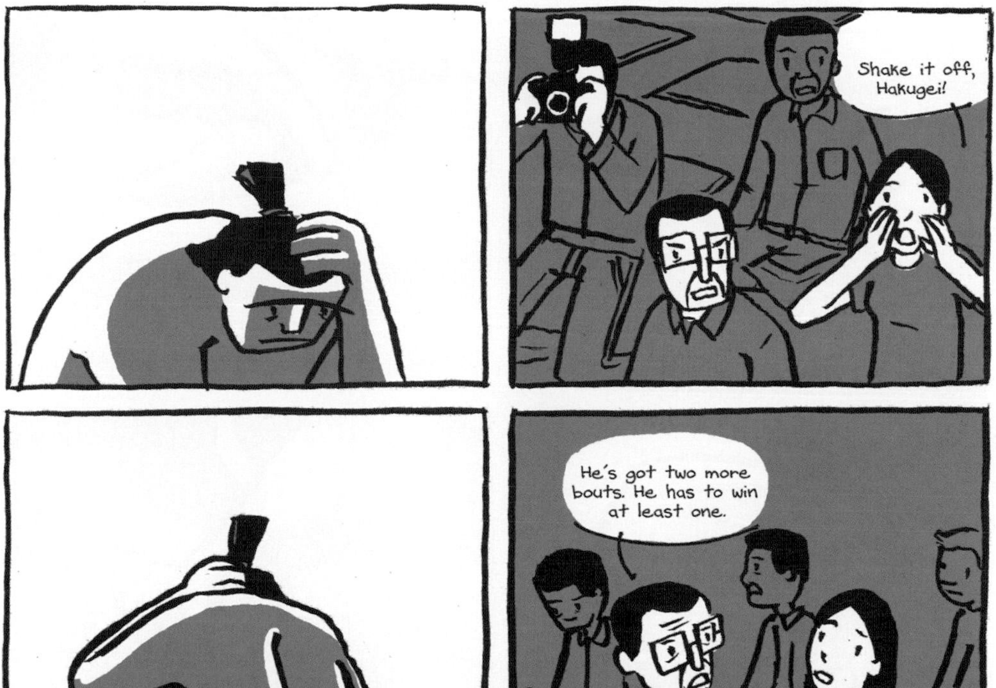
Shake it off, Hakugei!
He's got two more bouts. He has to win at least one.

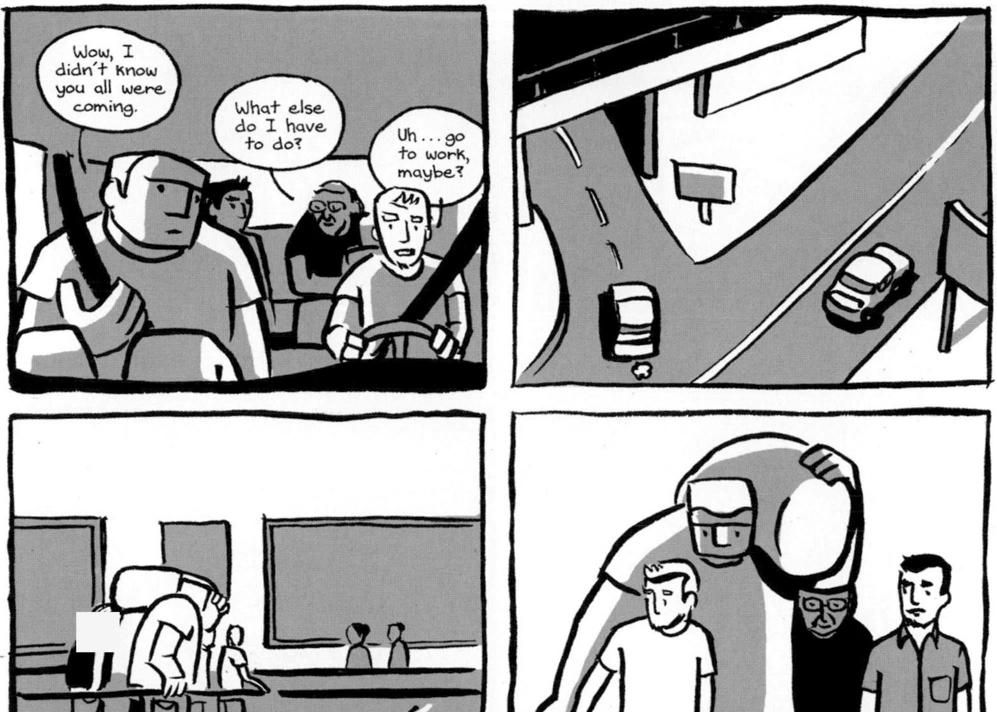

Wow, I didn't know you all were coming.
What else do I have to do?
Uh... go to work, maybe?
Gate twenty-nine.

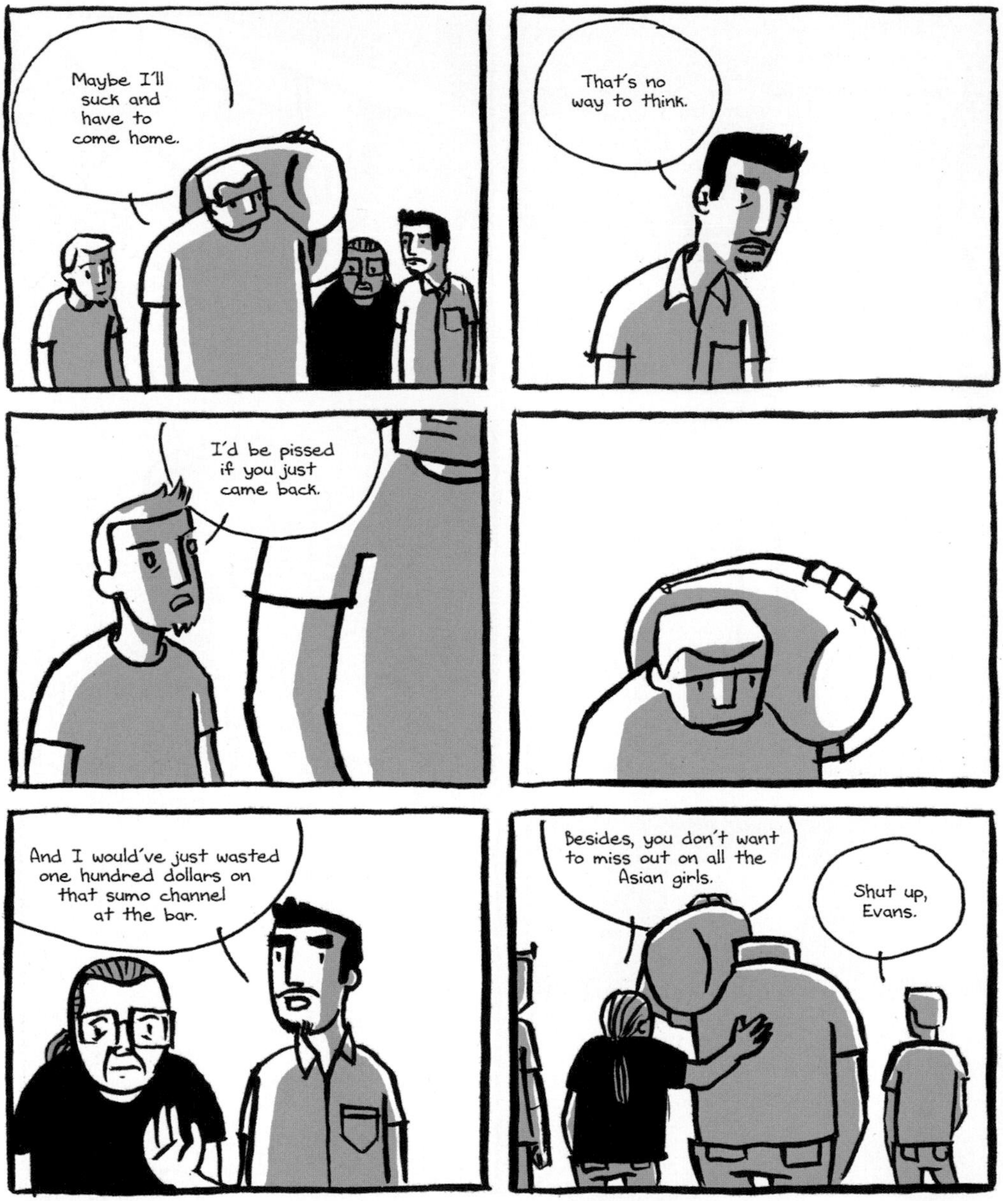
Maybe I'll suck and have to come home.
That's no way to think.
I'd be pissed if you just came back.
And I would've just wasted one hundred dollars on that sumo channel at the bar.
Besides, you don't want to miss out on all the Asian girls.
Shut up, Evans.

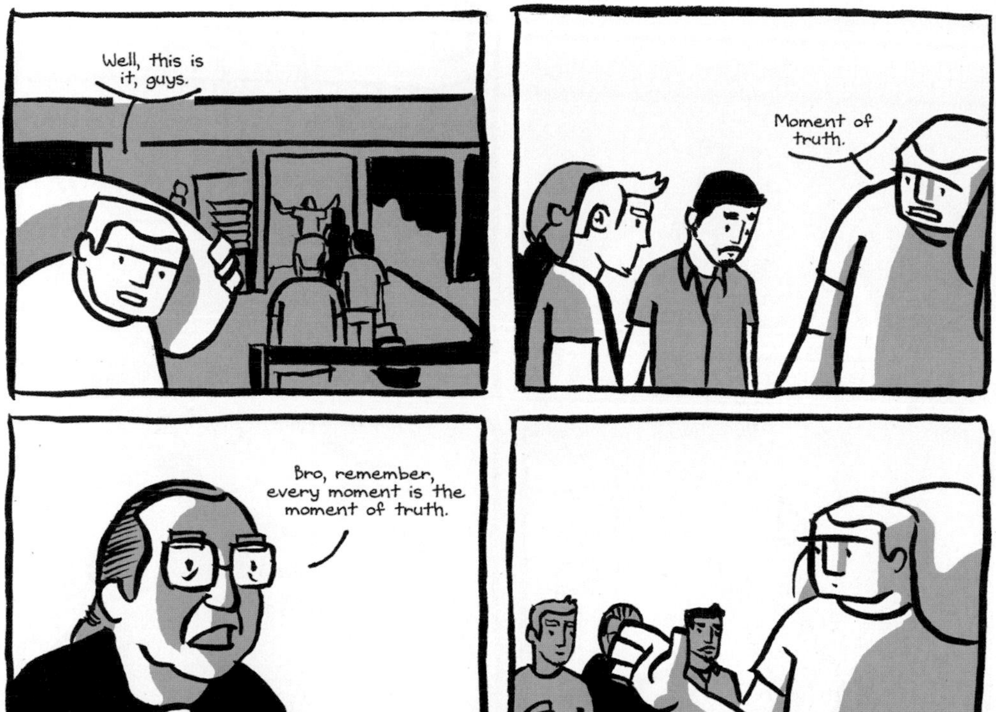
Well, this is it, guys.
Moment of truth.
Bro, remember, every moment is the moment of truth.
I think he'll be okay.

I think he'll be okay.

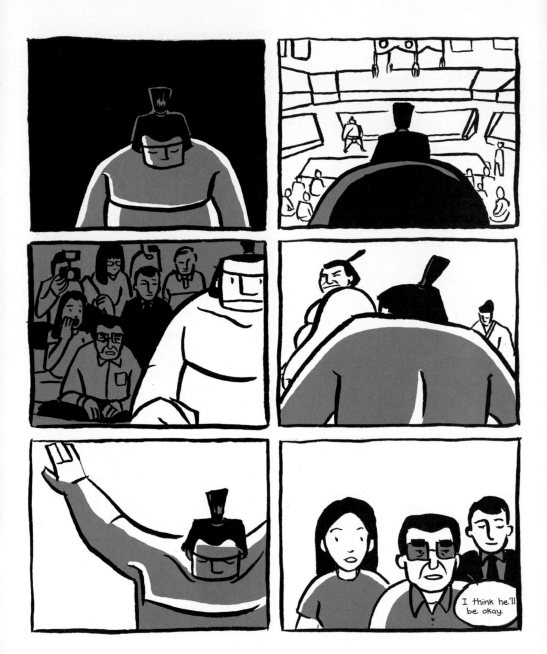

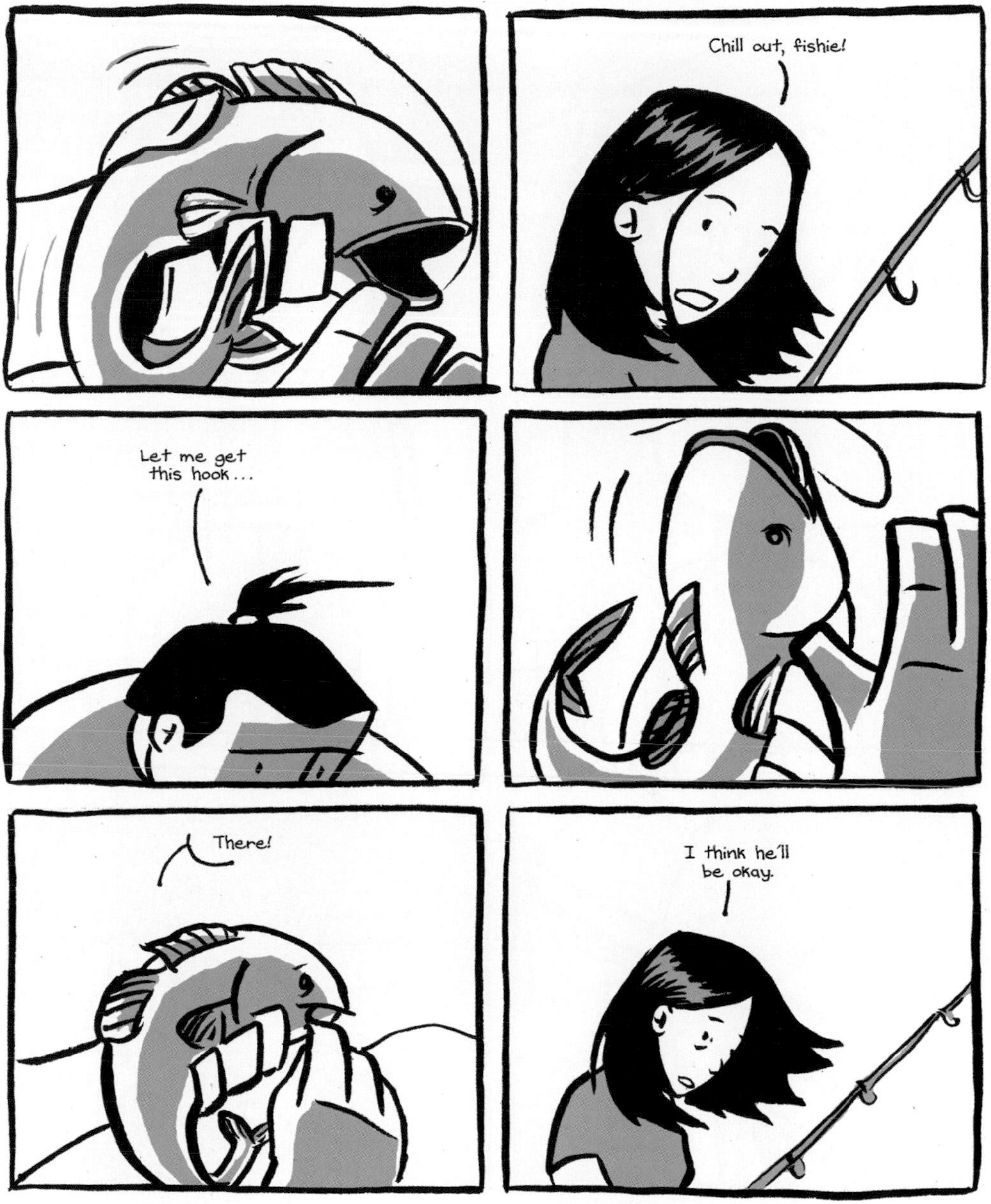
Chill out, fishie!
Let me get this hook...
There!
I think he'll be okay.

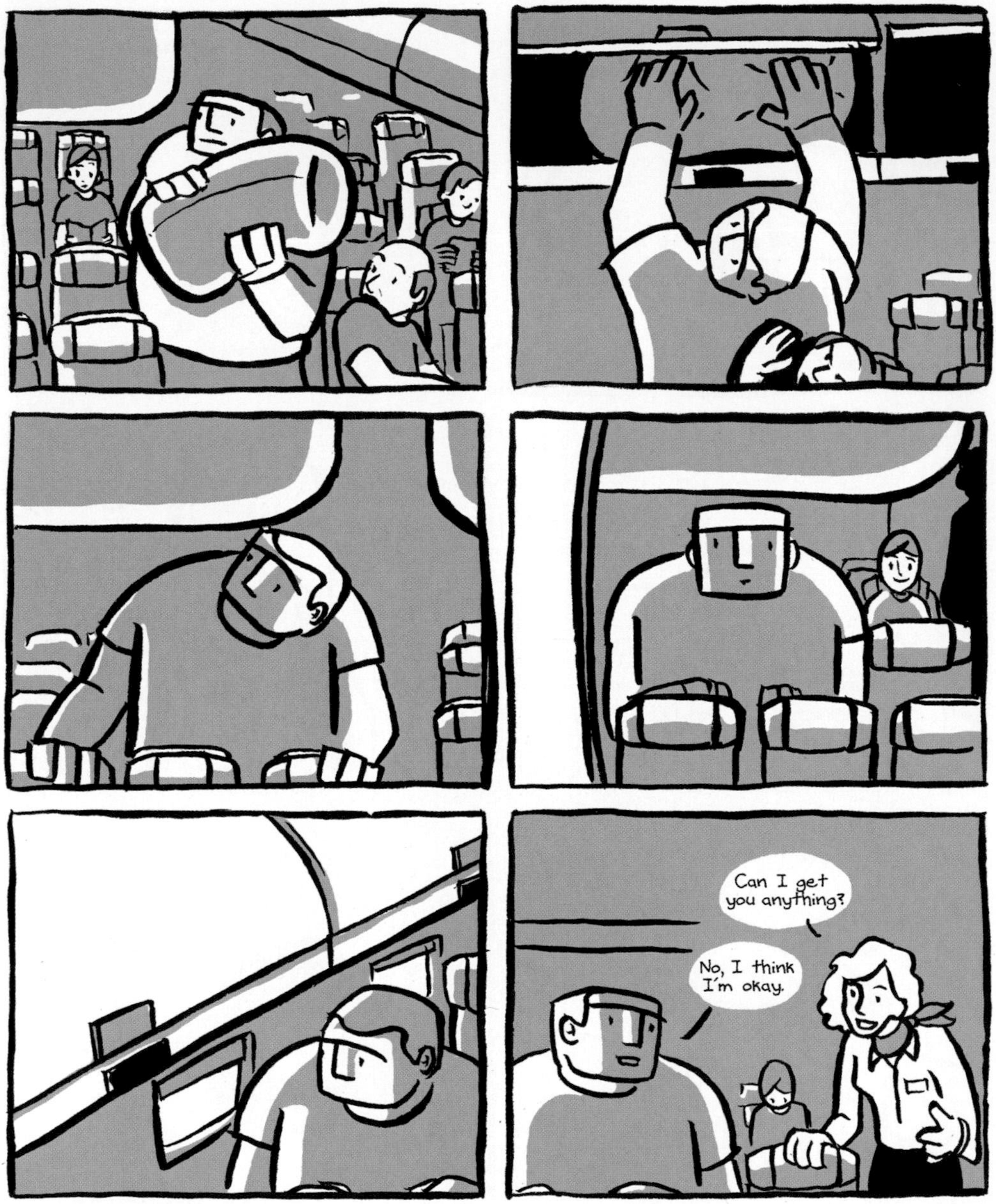
Can I get you anything?
No, I think I'm okay.

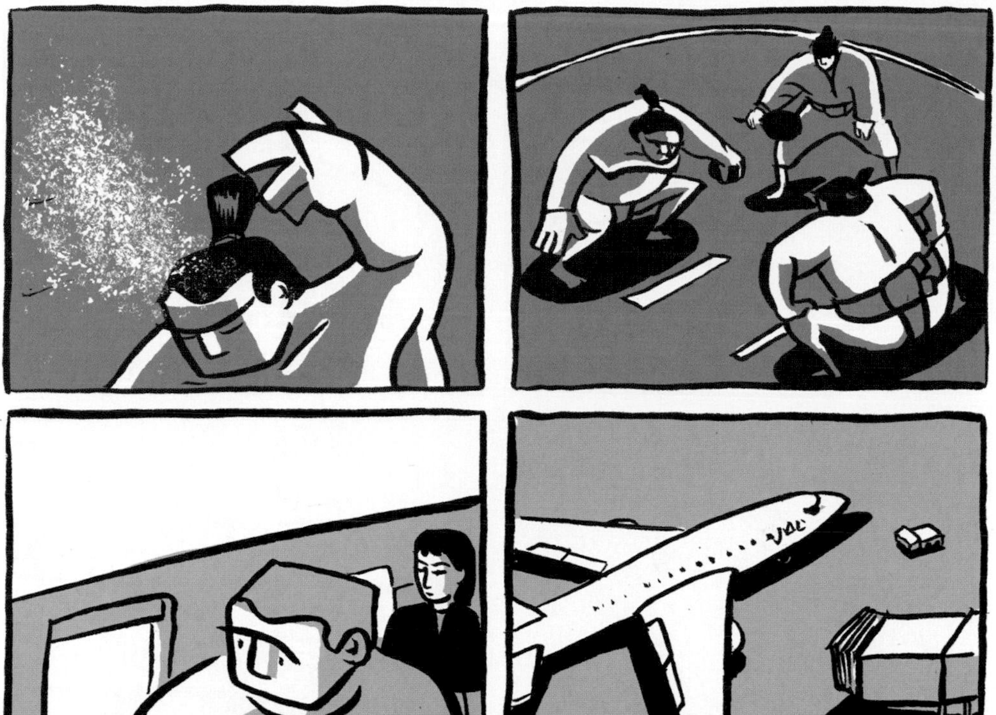
JAL

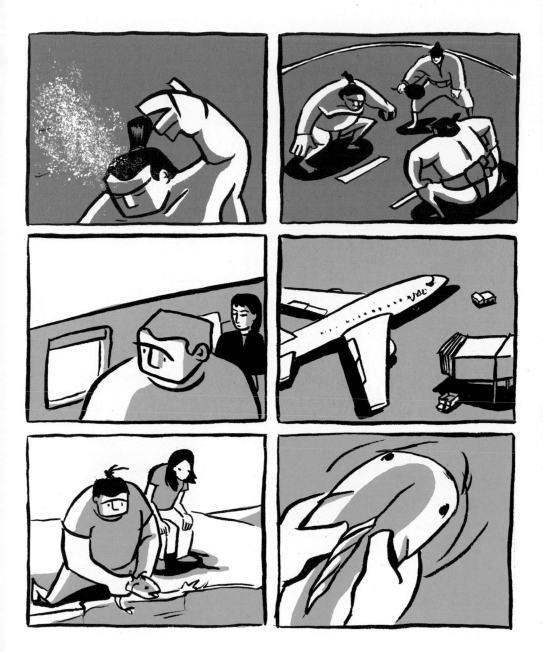

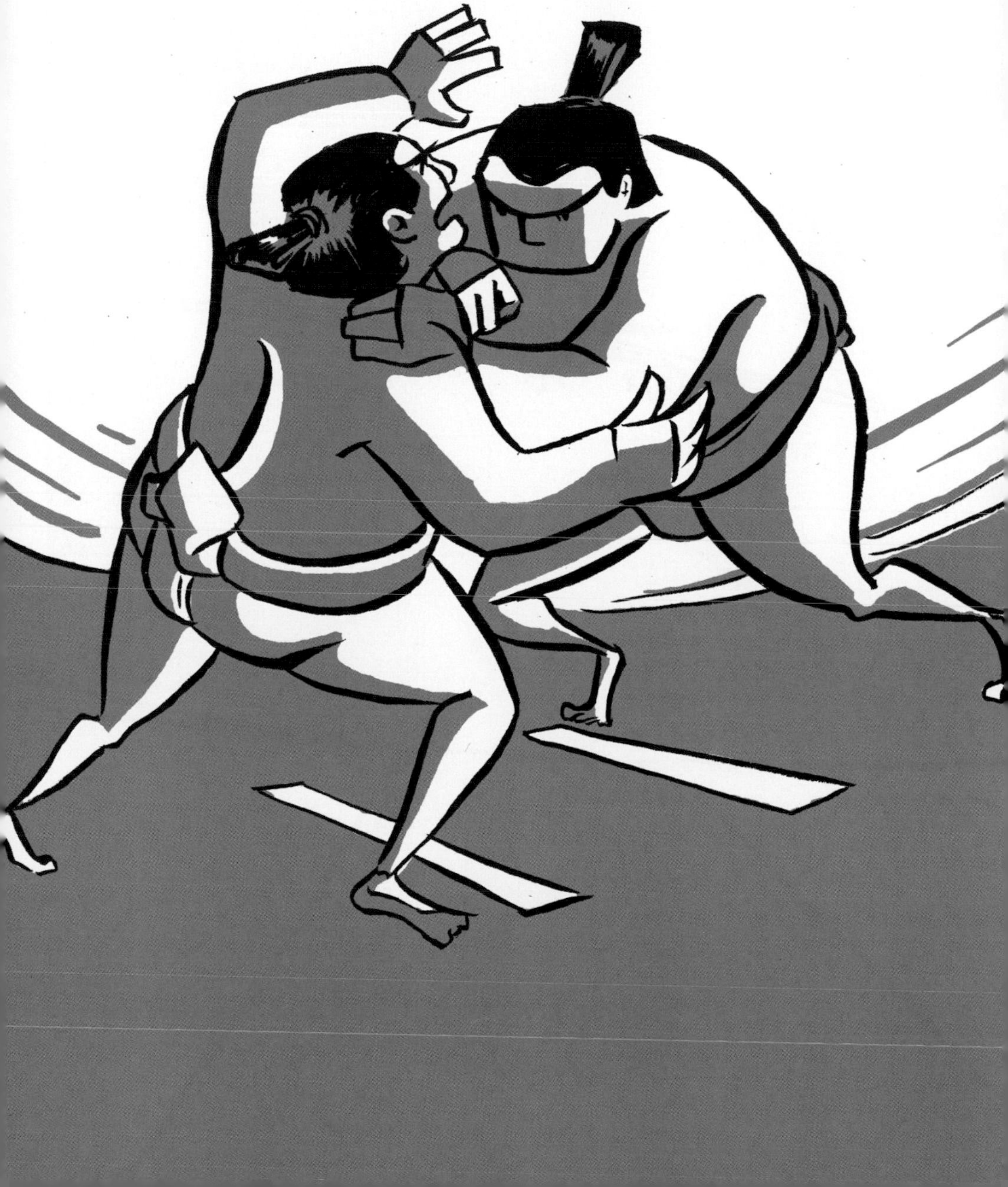

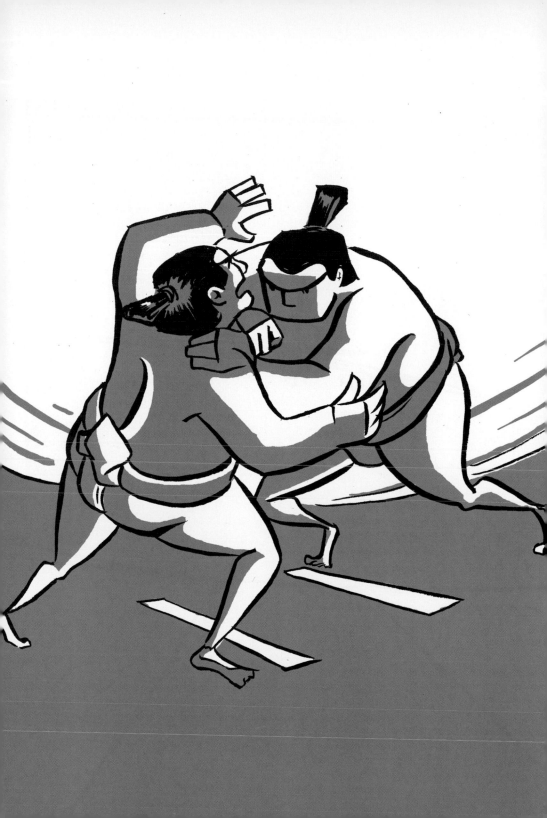

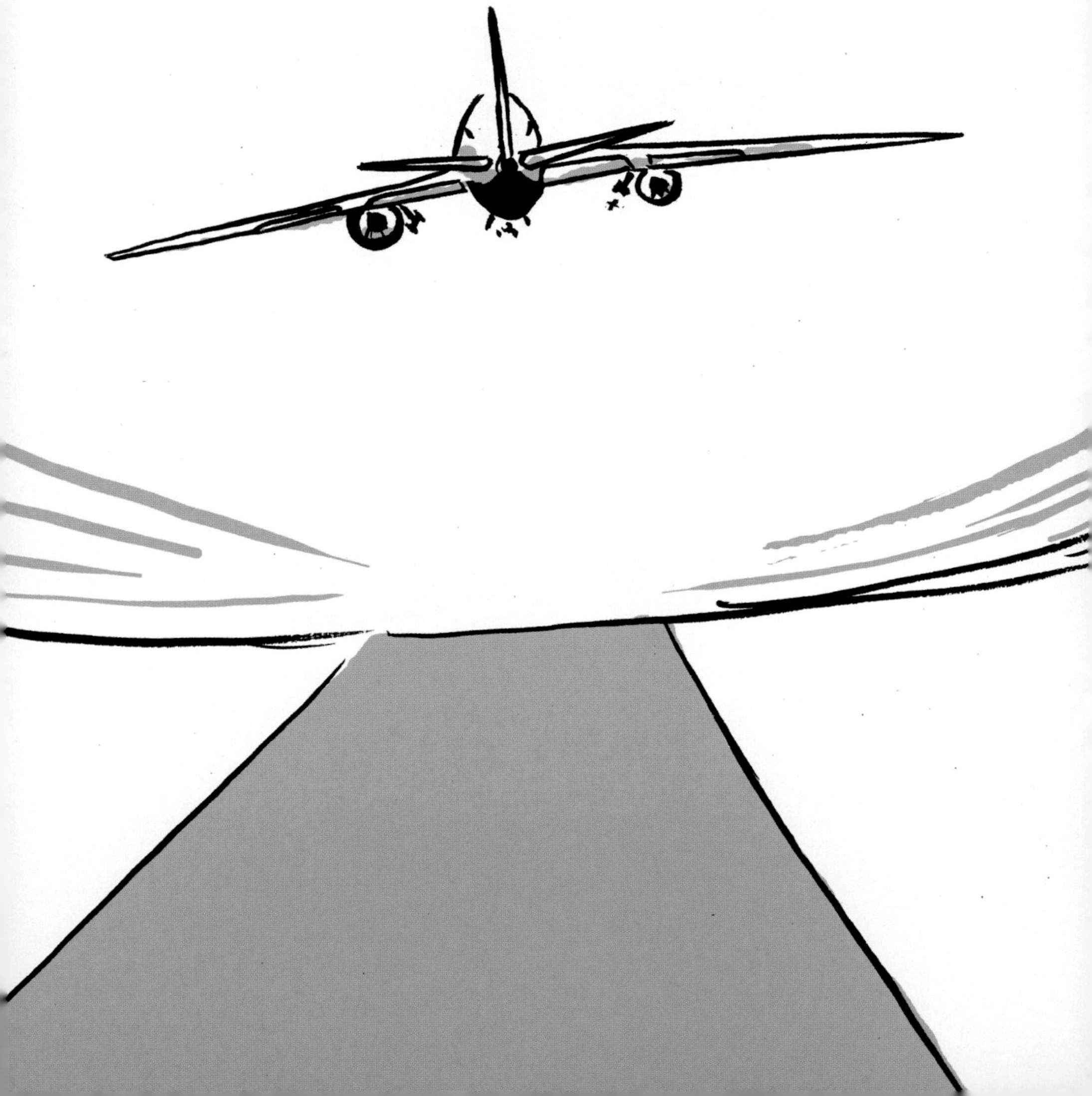

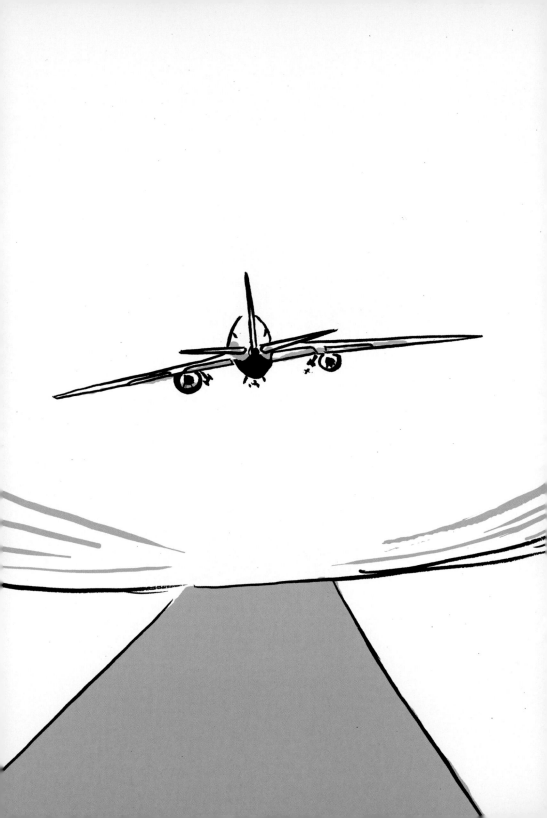

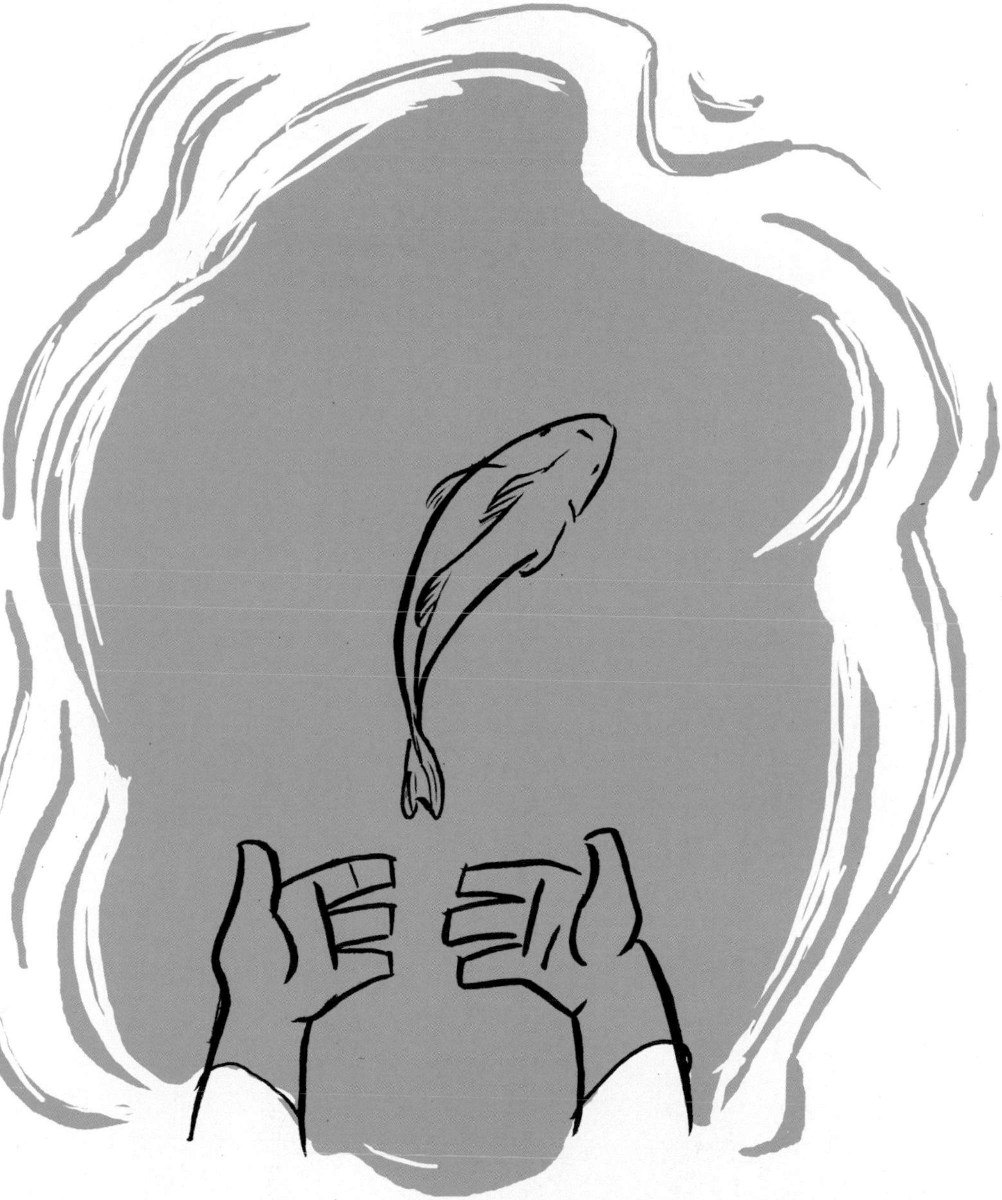

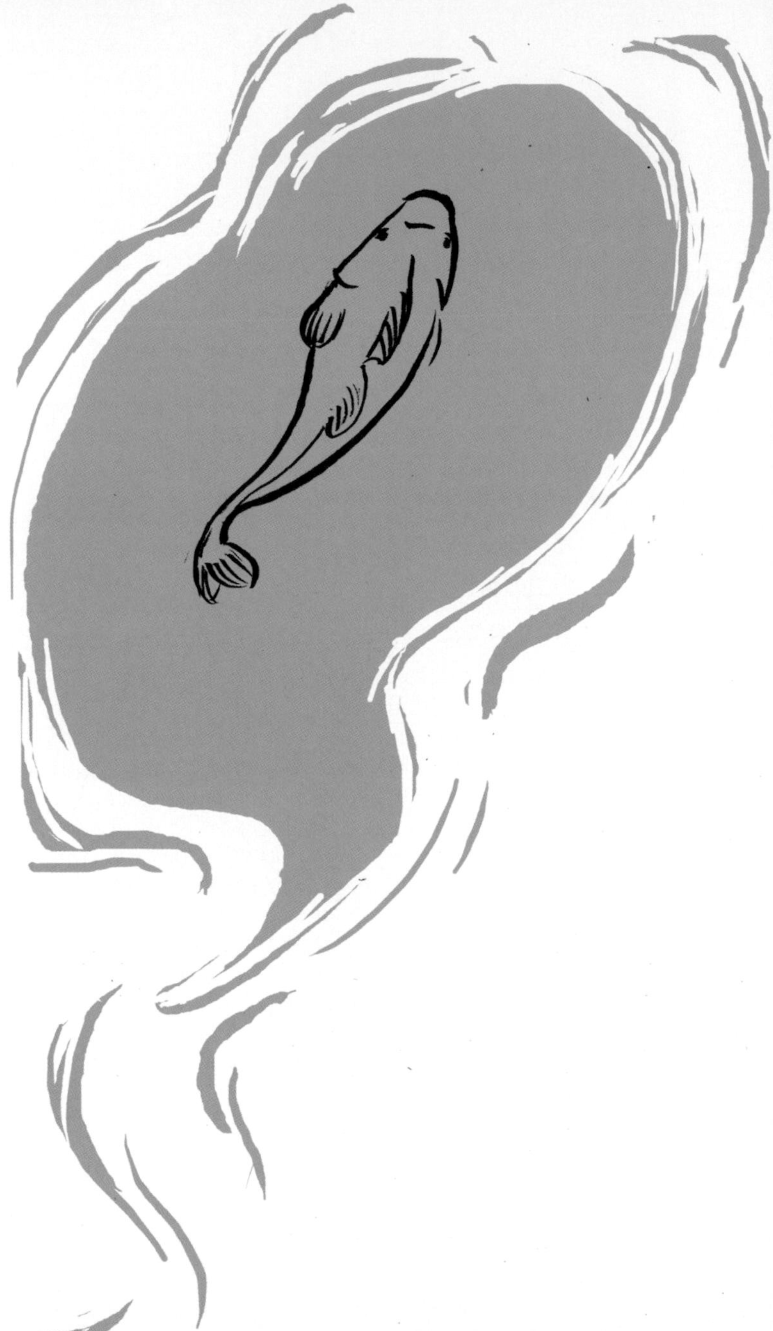

end.

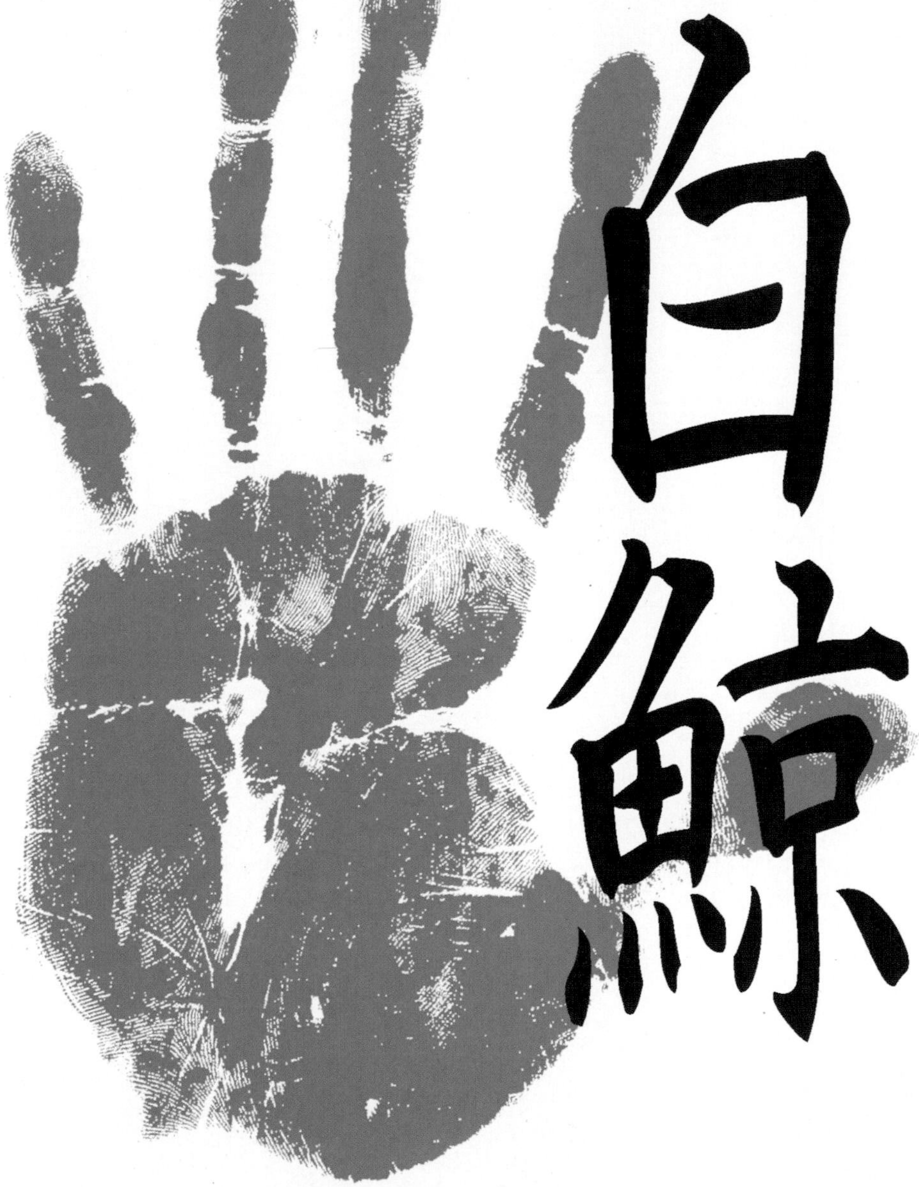
白鯨